DATE DUE

WINE, MURDER & BLUEBERRY SUNDAES

A Novel of Romance and Suspense

C.C. RISENHOOVER

McLennan HOUSE WAXAHACHIE

Published by
McLennan House, Inc.
206 South Rogers
Waxahachie, Texas 75165

Library of Congress Cataloging-in-Publication Data

Risenhoover, C.C., 1936–
WINE, MURDER & BLUEBERRY SUNDAES

I. Title.
ISBN 0-918865-04-2
Library of Congress Catalog Number: 86-62064

Manufactured in the United States of America
First Printing

To Her

PROLOGUE

I cannot honestly tell myself that I had no control over the situation, that I was merely a victim of circumstances. To do so would be a lie. In truth, for the better part of my life, I've always considered myself the master of my own destiny.

There have been times, of course, when the fates have dealt me some rather cruel blows. But none I couldn't handle. I've always thought of myself as having this inner strength, a mental bent superior to that of most men.

However, I really don't think such a situation could have occurred had I not determined my high and noble purpose in life was to be a university professor. For one thing, had I not been on a college campus, my range of acquaintances would have been different.

As to my worthiness in aspiring to the noble profession of university professor, from the first I have had some difficulty in considering myself qualified. It's not a matter of education, intelligence or experience, but rather that I think that such a high and noble calling requires a person to be almost Christ-like in his dealings. God knows, I miss the boat on that score. I do have principles, but they fall far short of a New Testament level.

I suppose I could attempt to justify my teaching and ethics on the lack of commitment exhibited by my colleagues, but to do so would be neither fair nor honest. How I respond to my purpose, to my reason for being, is a personal thing. I cannot justify my inadequacies or inconsistancies on the basis of what others do or don't do.

I worry because the way my teaching affects young minds is an awesome responsibility, one with which I probably never will feel all that comfortable.

But all that aside, it is still difficult for me to realize that I allowed the situation to occur; that I became so caught up in the emotion of the thing that it consumed me like a fire out of control.

1

It is generally hot and humid when registration for the fall semester begins. In Dallas, September is usually just an extension of the heat of August, though the latter part of the month may bring the promise of cooler nights in October. How the early settlers to this part of Texas endured some summers without the aid of air-conditioning, why they even wanted to, has always been a mystery to me.

Still, in spite of a smoldering sun that cracks crevices in unwatered earth, there is something exciting and refreshing about registration and the beginning of a new semester. It is a time of promise, of change, of new commitment by both old and new students.

It is even a time of faculty rededication.

I recall that I felt particularly good about the new semester, even when called on to pull a double shift during registration. In fact, I felt so good that I had difficulty maintaining my usual degree of irritability toward the university's grounds crew, whose lawn sprinklers seem always to target the sidewalks instead of the grass. Nevertheless, in spite of the grounds keepers' incompetence, the campus generally has the appearance of a botanical garden. I credit this to God being tolerant of fools and the university president for being the most image-conscious man alive.

The trees and shrubs are always perfectly pruned and, when weather permits, a bright array of flowers sparkle under the Texas sun.

Anyway, though there had been no rain showers for days, I still had to slosh through puddles of water and had to dodge deadly aim of beserk sprinklers when en route to the building where registration was taking place. Even with the best moves from my football playing days, I did not go unscathed; which didn't surprise me. I long ago determined that it is impossible to run through a rain forest without getting a few drops on you.

Of course, I was not the only one with wet clothes and shoes. Many students had also become victims of the diabolical grounds crew.

When inside the building, I recall that freezer-like air-conditioning blowing against the wetness of my clothes caused me to remember the university's free flu shot program for faculty. I wondered when it would begin.

"Brian, you really ought to take your clothes off before showering," David McPherson said with a laugh. "Has the grounds crew been after you again?"

McPherson is a fellow faculty member and best friend. In fact, it was Dave who recommended me for my current position.

I grinned and replied, "I guarantee you, Dave, I'm going to get those guys. That's going to be a priority item this year."

He changed the subject by asking, "Where have you been all summer?"

"Oh, not much of anywhere. I did a little fishing, took a couple of short trips, but mostly just laid around the pool."

While I was taking a seat behind the registration table and next to Dave, he continued with, "Betty and I tried to call you several times. We wanted to take you out to dinner, especially on your birthday." Betty is Dave's wife.

I laughed. "There are some things that are best forgotten. My birthday is one of them." The summer had delivered my thirty-ninth.

"Don't complain to me," Dave responded with a chuckle. "I'm three years up on you. But I have to say that I've never felt better."

I'm not sure what else we talked about that day. Registration procedures, student complaints and problems kept up pretty busy. I do know that Dave and Betty had been very concerned about my well-being, primarily my state of mind. For that matter, they're still concerned; probably always will be.

It had, at the time, been two years since the divorce. I had not taken rejection well, though my indiscretions were the reason my ex-wife had shown me the door.

There's a tendency to blame the disruption in my life on the middle-age crazies. However, looking back I have to admit that part of the problems that occurred had resulted from my immaturity. For too many years everything had gone too much my way.

Though I was born to relatively poor parents and raised in a small Texas town, my abilities in high school athletics catapulted me into considerable regional prominence. The ability to run with and throw a football, the ability to pitch and hit a baseball, were luckily the criteria necessary to offset poor parents in small town society.

During my junior and senior years in high school, my steady was the bank president's daughter. Had my athletic stature been less, or even nonexistent, it's doubtful that she would have given me the time of day.

Not that I was ugly or anything of that nature. I was, instead, considered to be quite handsome. Even now, fellow faculty members claim the reason so many coeds clamor to get into my classes has nothing to do with subject matter, but rather with my good looks and eligibility.

Be that as it may, poverty overshadows good looks in a small town, so it was definitely athletic ability that got me the banker's daughter.

Maybe poverty is too harsh a word. The facts are that my parents provided me more than enough good food to eat, along with decent clothes and shelter. My father was a hard-working man, just not a great money manager. We did live on the wrong side of the tracks.

Neither my girlfriend, her father or mother ever set foot inside our house. That way, they could at least delude themselves into thinking that my family's lifestyle was better than average.

Sports also enabled me to get decent-paying weekend and summer jobs, which financed my social life.

When the college offers came, they were, of course, to play football. My sports love was baseball, but football is king in Texas.

Though I was considered a great high school quarterback, I never felt I achieved all that much in the college game. I could blame my underachieving on inferior coaching but, in truth, I just couldn't get serious enough about the sport. I was not the easiest person to discipline and, because I enjoyed the wilder side of life, was never in the best of condition during the seasons I played.

Nevertheless, my team appeared in a bowl game each of the three years I was a starter, and I actually began to believe that I might be God's gift to the National Football League. A brief stint with the Houston Oilers ended that delusion, along with the idea that I was so good that conditioning wasn't necessary.

During my senior year of college, I had met and married Lisa Marie Martin. She was a sophomore at the time and her parents, who were in the upper socioeconomic strata, were quite vocal in their objections to our union.

Dave McPherson was my best man. Though older, he was in my class because he had served a hitch in the Marine Corps before entering college.

Lisa immediately rewarded my affection by getting pregnant. So, when the Oilers decided my knees weren't up to NFL standards, I had a wife and baby son to support. Sure, I had a college degree, but it was in journalism; not the kind of profession to provide the big paychecks I thought Lisa expected.

I misjudged, misread, her terribly. By the time I discovered my error, it was too late.

While in college there was no problem in getting money. When I had a financial problem that couldn't be handled with my regular pay for being on the team, I merely told a coach. A day or two later, one of the team's supporters would unceremoniously hand me an envelope containing what I needed.

Up until Houston cut me, all my needs had for years been provided because I was a jock. It was a shock to suddenly realize that I no longer had a service to sell. The Oilers did pay off my contract, which was small potatoes by today's standards, but we did have a little money on which to survive. But there wasn't enough to buy a business or anything like that.

Dave McPherson had enrolled in the graduate journalism program at Columbia, and suggested that I do the same. I told him, however, that neither school nor New York appealed to me. Of course, at the time I was too worried about finances to even consider additional schooling.

A few days after nixing the school idea, I was thumbing through the classified of the newspaper and spotted the Central Intelligence Agency ad. The very fact that the Agency advertised intrigued me. For a small town boy who had grown up reading about and watching movie exploits of America's spies, the possibility of any kind of job with the Agency was exciting.

So, I applied.

Admittedly, even after going through all the tests and screening, I was surprised at being accepted.

What followed was a lengthy training period, during which I did not have much time for Lisa or a small son. I was home long enough to once again get her pregnant. The new arrival was a daughter, which made Lisa very happy.

I won't go into great detail concerning time spent with the Agency. It's sufficient to say that I was not a trench coat type operative. I never went to exotic places, nor did I ever encounter beautiful women spies. More often than not my clothing was camouflage-colored military issue. My field of operation was usually behind enemy lines, real or imagined, and had I been caught I would probably have been executed on the spot, or tortured to death. My assigned travels took me to the real armpits of the world.

My initial stay with the Agency was for three years. I then got a job with a newspaper, attended college at night and earned an advanced degree.

Of course, you never really get free of the Agency. I was frequently used for short duration assignments that didn't interfere all that much with my job or schooling. And after a couple of semi-civilian years, I was talked into returning to the Agency for a special assignment in Southeast Asia.

Anyway, my life for several years was one of constant change. I would spend time working for the Agency, then time working for the paper. It was more unsettling to Lisa than to my two employers or me, but it wasn't really the reason for the divorce.

By the way, as for what the newspaper's management knew regarding my absences, my cover was that of a major in Air Force Intelligence. Management thought that by allowing me to do my duty, the paper was simply fulfilling a responsibility to an Air Force reservist.

I cannot now recall how I felt when Lisa filed for divorce. I now know that I was never in love with her, primarily because when I met her I was too much in love with myself. I was so immature that, in a sense, she had to raise me as well as the children.

It was after she filed for divorce that Dave McPherson recommended me for a faculty position at the university where he was teaching. When it was offered, I of course accepted, which led to the situation that eventually occurred.

From a personal standpoint, my first two years at the university were a bit shaky. I was still locked in the throes of depression because of the divorce, and because of what I thought was an incomprehensible and unnecessary tragedy for my children. It was much later that I realized that children are much more resilient than adults.

At the beginning of the semester in which the situation occurred, I had pretty well licked the problems caused by the divorce and, for all practical purposes, had made peace with myself. That had been my project over the summer, which is why Dave and Betty had experienced difficulty in locating me.

During the summer I had heeded a compulsion and returned to the site of my birth. That blessed event had taken place in an unpainted farmhouse that belonged to my grandparents. I have only limited memory of the house. It burned to the ground many years ago, and even its ashes have been scattered by the wind. The remaining evidence of the structure is the skeleton of a fireplace chimney that stands silhouetted against the sky.

Silver maple trees, their leaves always shimmering in

the softest of breezes, are still scattered about the grounds where the house once stood. However, brush and high grass have triumphed over what was once a well-kept yard and fields, much like evil is often victorious over good. The big, proud oak that stood in the front yard with branches raised heavenward, had fallen and was in a state of decay.

I recall that on my visit, which was in last August, I visualized the fall; the season that deteriorates into winter and makes any thinking person aware of the brevity of all things, especially his or her own life. I further recall that the visit to my birthplace filled me with melancholy and regret, thoughts of what might have been.

I now realize such thoughts were a fitting prelude to the situation that occurred in the fall.

There is a time in every man's life when his spirit cries out for change, for new direction, for meaning. For me, that time was most evident when I returned to my birthplace. It was a time of searching for what might have been, but more important, for what might be.

It is what might be that keeps a man searching for and pursuing something as elusive and intangible as a meaning to life. What still might be is what keeps him striving toward some calling he is incapable of interpreting. It is that anticipation of the future that enables a man's imagination to soar.

Expectation.

That's what it's all about.

The situation that occurred in the fall was unexpected, but it gave me a new perspective on expectation.

I reiterate that the farmhouse in which I was born

belonged to my grandparents, hardy pioneer stock who asked no quarter from the harsh land and gave none. They asked from the land only a meager return for the sweat and toil they put into it.

I miss them.

My grandfather, I admired. My grandmother, I adored.

For some reason, though, standing there in what used to be their yard, I remembered Roland. This is a rather latent memory, a vague face in the recesses of my mind. But he was a memory I have carried with me all these years; a memory that demands understanding, explanation, interpretation.

Roland had died. He died before tasting much of the sweetness of life, or before he experienced struggle, heartache, and pain.

He died when five years old. I was four at the time. He was my friend, and the first person I ever knew who died. His death is, perhaps, the reason why I've always had difficulty being close to anyone.

I recall that standing there I couldn't help but wonder, why Roland? Why not me? It was a question that has popped up in my mind many times over the years.

I was startled from such thought processes by a movement to my left. A snake slithered away from my intrusion. I wondered if there was any significance to seeing the snake, then became angry at myself for trying to interpret symbolically everything I saw or heard in relation to my life.

Hell, I'm just not that important.

For some reason, though, I'm always looking for the

symbolic significance; the result, perhaps, of too many English classes.

Anyway, since depression about the deterioration of my birthplace already had me in its grasp, I decided to visit the old ranch house my parents rented shortly after Roland's death. I'd spent a couple of happy years there.

My depression intensified when I saw the emptiness and decay of what was the freshly-painted white two-story house of my memory. Its paint was now cracked and peeling. Ugly vines climbed the front porch columns and walls, choking all life from it.

The fields around the house were empty of cattle and horses. There was no sign of life anywhere, not even a grasshopper jumping or a bee buzzing.

I recall that my imagination ran rampant. I imagined that some invisible force was trying to destroy all evidence of my past, making it seem as if I had never existed. I felt that my mind was caught up in a period of time that never ended, because it had never really begun.

It is hard to believe that I actually longed for the sound of bumblebees, those hairy-looking social creatures that once had an affinity for the front yard; that had negated my play there because they frightened me. But there were no bees, no sound of them. There was only an eerie quiet that made me wish for some sound, something alive and moving; something to make me believe that I once was, that my past was not just a dream.

But even the wind refused to blow softly enough to rustle a leaf or blade of grass.

I walked southward, down toward the creek behind the house, recalling the many happy hours I had spent there with a friend. It bothered me that I could not remember his name or face. I could remember Roland, so why not him?

We had spent summer mornings making arrows for homemade bows. We had spent afternoons at the creek shooting the arrows at watersnakes. The snakes were never in any real danger.

On that August day, I had stood on the creekbank and saw no snakes. It was a hot, still, lifeless day, and there was no movement anywhere.

I walked back to the house and thought about how it had once rung with music and laughter, especially on the weekends. It had been a happy place, a place of parties, dancing, and drinking. My parents may have been short on money, but not on ways to have a good time.

I sat in my car for maybe ten or fifteen minutes, pondering the terrain and reflecting on the ridiculousness of my mental state. Here I was, a man who had been given many opportunities, who had seized a good share of them, and who for two years had been feeling sorry for himself. I also thought about the human hopelessness I'd seen in some countries.

Then I started laughing at myself, for the kind of idiocy I'd been practicing.

Granted, you can't go home again, but an occasional trip back to the past is a good thing. The good memories, those are the important things from the past. The anticipation of what lies ahead, that's the importance of tomorrow.

On that hot August day, I resolved some of the problems that had been plaguing me; the divorce, how to deal with my children, and my goals for the future. And it wasn't a matter of pushing the bad out of my mind and merrily skipping into the future. It was, rather, a matter of determining to cope with what had happened, to treasure the good memories and to be conscious of and to try to not make the same mistakes again.

Maybe such resolve was just a matter of elapsed time in regard to the divorce; I don't know. I just know that I spent a lot of time alone that summer. As I said, this was why Dave and Betty McPherson couldn't reach me.

Dave and I visited quite a bit during registration, but I didn't tell him I had resolved some of my problems since he'd last seen me. It wasn't the sort of thing we talked about. But if I hadn't begun the semester with an improved attitude, the situation would not have occurred.

2

I became very much aware of the girl on the first day of class. It was the same day Dean Reginald Masters allegedly committed suicide. Of course, I didn't believe for a second that the pompous little ass had hanged himself.

But to more important matters first.

I had already begun my lecture when she entered the room. Her arrival created a stir among the male students, and for good reason. I recall thinking then that she was the most beautiful woman I had ever seen.

In discussing her beauty, though, I don't want to talk in the past tense. After all, I consider her even more beautiful today than when I first saw her, which was about three weeks ago. Or was it four? With what has transpired in the past few weeks, I've had difficulty with continuity.

Anyway, to describe any beautiful woman is a task that demands knowledge of every appropriate word in the dictionary. And although I've mastered much such absurdity, where she is concerned I find myself still lacking in vocabulary.

It is possible to describe a perfectly shaped face, dark

green eyes that pierce a man's soul, and a mouth so sensuous it kindles unbelievable passion. Her skin, too, has perfect tone, and her long, flowing brown hair puts one in a hypnotic trance. She has a softness and specialness about her that I have found in no other woman.

To say I have been smitten would be an understatement. Of course, I would not want her to know the depth of my feelings. If she knew, it would make me too vulnerable, a condition I do not enjoy.

On that first day I saw her, I recall being filled with regret at the years that separated us. From my perspective, those years were like an impenetrable wall, one whose height reached the heavens and whose thickness was as endless as the universe.

Before you think me tottering on the brink of senility, I reiterate that during the summer I had suffered my thirty-ninth birthday. And here was a woman, beautiful though she was, who was only twenty. In the years that separated us, there had been time for a couple of wars. There had also been time for me to have a couple of children, who were just a few years shy of her age.

Since my divorce, it had never occurred to me to express a romantic interest in anyone under thirty. There have been some younger women who showed an interest in me, but I dismissed their attention. As my friends often laughingly relate, I am more the hero of the post-deb set.

Also, there has been my idea of a student-teacher relationship, corny as it may sound, which has prohibited taking advantage of my position. I reiterate that I consider teaching a serious responsibility, and strive to do nothing that would bring discredit to the profession.

After the first day's class she approached me and said, "Dr. Stratford, I wanted to apologize for being late. My name is Deseret Antares."

I smiled. "Don't worry about it. And I'm not a doctor. Just call me Brian."

She returned the smile and replied, "That doesn't seem very respectful, calling a professor by his first name."

"Oh, I don't think it's disrespectful. You obviously missed my remarks at the beginning of class."

"I'm afraid so."

"Well, to give you a synopsis of my opening verbiage, all students in my classes are treated as adults and will be expected to act as such. Thus, we should be on a first name basis. I don't want to be formal or put myself on a level where students feel uncomfortable discussing problems with me."

"I was told you were different," she said.

I laughed. "I don't know whether that's a compliment or not."

She smiled again. "It's a compliment."

"Well, I appreciate it."

"I just wanted to make sure you hadn't counted me absent."

"I didn't even bother to take roll," I said. "I'll take it a couple of times next week to make sure everyone who signed up for the course is properly registered, but after that it's up to you as to whether or not you attend class. Roll call is a senseless exercise for adults."

She gave an appreciative laugh. "You really are different."

I saw no need to respond to her comment, but changed the subject with, "Your name, it's unusual. It's even beautiful, if that's an appropriate description for a name."

"Thank you. My mother says she named me Deseret because she wishes her mother had given her that name. Of course, as you might guess, most of my friends call me Dez."

"It figures," I said. "I'll call you Deseret or Dez, whichever you prefer. I'll even call you Ms. Antares, if you want me to be more formal."

She smiled. "I think I'd like for you to call me Dez, too."

"Dez it is then."

I'm not sure about the rest of our conversation, which was fairly brief. I did get the idea, however, that she was reluctant to end it. I know there was reluctance on my part, because she stirred emotions I didn't know I even possessed.

3

Their first brief encounter had also stirred Deseret, and she was quite disturbed because of it.

This isn't the way it's supposed to be, she thought.

Indeed, it wasn't. She wanted the professor to be interested in her, but her plan did not include a romantic interest in him. While Brian Stratford could not recall ever having seen her until that first class day of the fall semester, she had both seen him and had considerable knowledge about him.

In spite of such knowledge, he had disarmed her; not only with his smile and easy manner, but also with his piercing eyes. She now knew what some of the girls in the sorority meant when they said he had bedroom eyes, and it had nothing to do with their hazel color.

He looked much younger than his years, too. Had she not known he was thirty-nine, she would have guessed him to be thirty; even with his salt and pepper colored hair, which she thought was a little too short. She figured it might be a result of his military background, about which she had heard considerable speculation from students. There was a lot of mystery to the man, which she found quite intriguing.

His bearing certainly spoke of military training, the standing-at-attention-like posture that made him seem taller than six-feet-two-inches. Lean and well-porportioned, he didn't look as though he weighed two hundred pounds, either.

Also catching her attention were the perfectly straight teeth, along with a tanned face that looked as though it had never witnessed a blemish.

Darn, he would have to look like a Greek god, she thought, then reevaluated her assessment and surmised that he didn't look like one of those mythical characters at all. He was more rugged looking, more the outdoor type.

If she had earlier doubts, the close-up encounter erased them. He was a man she would be proud to be seen with, no matter where and no matter what the difference in their ages.

Now, she wished that she could have met him under less devious circumstances. She regretted that her decision to meet him, to enroll in his class, was the result of a wager with some of her sorority sisters. They had laid down the challenge, said he wouldn't date a student. They said that in the two years he had been at the university, numerous young women had given him every opportunity, but their success factor had been zero.

She had maintained that he hadn't met the right coed, which had resulted in a challenge from some of the girls. Now she wished she hadn't accepted it, because she would have preferred to have known him in a different context.

4

News of the dean's alleged suicide reached me late in the afternoon on that first day of class. Dave McPherson was the source.

"No way," I said.

"The police seem to be satisfied it was a suicide," Dave countered.

"The police didn't know him," I argued. "That pompous little ass was in his glory. There's no way he would give up another year of belittling the faculty in order to meet his maker. And I'm not crediting God with being his maker, either."

Dave laughed. "Of course, it's just hearsay, but you'd better hope the police keep thinking it's a suicide. If they decide it's murder, then you'll be a prime suspect."

It was my turn to laugh. "If I'd punched his ticket, I'd have done it in a more creative way."

"That I can believe."

"Where, and at what time, did this so-called suicide take place?" I asked.

"His secretary found him this morning about nine."

"Hanging around his office, I suppose?"

Dave laughed. "That's bad, really bad. But yes, that's

where she found him. The poor woman's in shock."

"She's probably overwrought with joy. I guess the rope was attached to the ceiling fan, huh?"

"Hey, you are a good suspect."

"It doesn't take a Sherlock Holmes to realize that the most logical place in his office to tie a rope is the extension pole on the ceiling fan. I do assume he was hanged with a rope, not a clothes hanger or something like that?"

"I heard he used parachute cord," Dave replied.

"Now, why in the hell would he have any parachute cord?" I asked.

"Anyone can get parachute cord. Maybe he got it from an army surplus store."

"I know anyone can get parachute cord, but can you really imagine Reginald going into an army surplus store? If Neiman-Marcus doesn't sell it, I don't believe he bought it." My impression of the dean was that he was more image-conscious than the univesity's president. He wouldn't be seen in a Burger King or McDonald's, only in the finest restaurants, stores, and so on.

But Dave argued, "When a man's mentally disturbed, there's no telling what he might do."

"I sure can't argue with the mentally disturbed part, but I think Reginald was always mentally disturbed. Of course, I think anyone who has been at the university for five years is mentally disturbed. In fact, Dave, I'm a bit worried about you."

He grinned. "Yeah, Brian, you're the only sane one here, right?"

"That's about the size of it," I joked.

Dave returned the conversation to seriousness with, "I just can't think of anyone who would want to kill him."

"I can't think of anyone who wouldn't," I responded. "At least, anyone who knew him."

I'm not really a callous person, but I found it difficult to grieve for Dean Reginald Masters. I had made no secret of the fact that I detested the man. We'd had some dandy confrontations, but none that would have caused me to do away with him. I have a very strong reverence for life, any life. It is, perhaps, because I saw such disregard for it in Southeast Asia.

Anyway, while I couldn't grieve for him, I was sorry that he had come to such a sad end.

I think my lack of grief was shared by most faculty members, though in the aftermath of his death some would have you believe that they considered the dean as being close to the reincarnation of Jesus. As for me, in my memory he will also be a spiteful little man with adequate book knowledge and absolutely no common sense. If he had any virtues, they were hidden from me.

Admittedly, I am a bit prejudiced in my thinking. For example, in my opinion the criteria for being a college administrator is a large dose of idiocy, for which there is no known cure. To be a successful college administrator, one must learn to spend money as foolishly as the Congress. We elect that kind of stupidity, but in the case of college administrators, no one seems to know how or why they are spawned. Those of us in teaching simply know that the world has given birth to too many of them.

My problems with Reginald began when a secretary informed him that I was a rather liberated type, a womanizer who continually made advances on female students. She further stated that I was living with a coed at the time.

Her information was, of course, untrue. Several female students had made romantic overtures toward me, all of which I had rejected. But without so much as consulting me regarding the charges, Reginald conspired with the chairman of the journalism department to have me dismissed from the faculty. Had it not been for the departmental secretary alerting me to the skulduggery going on behind my back, the attempts of these hypocrites to destroy me might have gone unabated.

As it was, my training enabled me to secure a copy of the secret file that contained the charges against me. To say I was angry after reading them would be a gross understatement. In the heat of the moment, I did contemplate the possibility of helping Reginald and the chairman to hang themselves, side-by-side, with notes confessing to their homosexuality. Believe me, with the kind of methods I was taught, I could have secured those notes in their handwriting and wouldn't have left a mark on their bodies.

However, reason overcame anger. I am, after all, a civilized man whose psyche has been bent only slightly by war. I decided I wanted Reginald and the chairman alive and well, both knowing that I knew what they had attempted to do.

I confronted both of them, threatened legal action and made them crawfish.

When I attacked, my first reaction was to mount a counter offensive. I'm quite good at it, and, perhaps, even overdid it with Reginald and the chairman. However, since I had done everything in my power to be a model teacher, my feeling is that the attack on me gave me every right to be resentful and even vindictive.

After the confrontation, I guess you could say, in a sense, that I enjoyed having Reginald around; like a dog enjoys a fireplug. The same could be said regarding my attitude toward the chairman of the journalism department, who is a mirror image of Reginald.

He is a man with absolutely no experience in journalism, relies strictly on what he can read in books, most of which are written by persons just like him. If you're wondering as to how students can learn about the real world of journalism from someone like him, it beats the hell out of me.

Of course, one of the real problems in journalism education are the type persons teaching the discipline. Most have never had to prove themselves by actually working in the media. Most of them have never written any real stories, only ridiculous research papers that appear in journals that no one reads.

But I digress.

The day after the dean's death, a group of faculty members, including the chairman of the journalism department, came to my office and asked if I would look into the alleged suicide. I gave Dave McPherson, who was a member of the entourage, a nasty look. I figured he was responsible for stirring things up, and for dragging this unofficial committee to my office.

"I'm sure the police have checked everything out thoroughly," I lied. "And I thought everyone was convinced it was a suicide."

"Dave got me thinking about it, and now I'm not so sure," the chairman said.

I gave Dave another hard look. "Regardless, why ask someone like me to check into it?"

"You know," the chairman replied with a bemused look.

"No, I don't know," I countered.

"Your background," he clarified.

I started to ask, what about my background? Then I looked at the faces in the group, including Dave's and realized they all thought of me as a master spy turned teacher. The sports jacket I was wearing was, to them, a trench coat.

Of course, I had told none of them, including Dave, that I was CIA-connected. That had been a secret from the very first contact with the Agency. Even my ex-wife thought I was regular Air Force.

Real CIA operatives don't run around telling folks, even wives and best friends, about working for the Agency. It's not that they're ashamed of what they do, but simply a matter of the Agency frowning on such revelations.

Unfortunately, a check into my background is so unrevealing that it starts a person to wondering, thus to drawing some conclusions; which is probably what occurred when the university checked me out prior to employment. Some bureaucrat probably acted sinister when relating some Agency-concocted tale about my military experience.

Then there's Dave, who is always questioning me

about past periods of time when we were out of touch. My evasiveness has caused considerable suspicion on his part. I've never told him anything, but he's intelligent enough to have drawn all the right conclusions.

Anyway, there are some mysterious elements to my past, which cause people to talk. Dave is good about stirring up such conversation. Because he knows me so well, he thinks it's all pretty funny, my evasiveness and such. He's also quick to tell anyone who will listen that I'm the best investigative reporter he knows, with the postscript, "He ought to be. The CIA spent a fortune training him."

That's why I knew Dave had instigated the group's visit to my office. And more to get them out of my office than anything else, I agreed to look into the matter of the dean's death.

"Don't expect any miracles," I warned. "Any of you are just as capable of checking this out as I am."

My statement drew no response, only bemused looks.

The more I thought about my unofficial assignment, however, the more intrigued I became at the thought of investigating Reginald's death. I often suffer from acute attacks of boredom, so checking out the alleged suicide would enable me to offset some of my leisure-time depression.

Strange as it may seem, during some periods of boredom I actually miss war. That may sound crazy, war being what it is, but there are things about it that I like. I don't love it as General Patton did, but I do like it.

When you awake every morning thinking it may be your last day on earth, when you go to sleep at night thinking you may never again see the light of day, there is a greater appreciation for life. That's why I felt very alive in Vietnam.

If my teaching colleagues had only known my role in the war, they might have looked at me much differently. I commanded an elite force, which sounds better than commanding killers and assassins. Some of our own people called us such, but we simply considered ourselves as soldiers doing our duty. Killing was just part of that duty.

I can't see that it makes much difference if the killing is done from close range or with bombs from thirty thousand feet, though the latter is the way most Americans want to be involved.

Unfortunately, it just fell our lot to be the ones to use weapons like piano wire, knives, and small but sophisticated explosive devices. We were always traveling light and fast, usually with the enemy breathing down our necks.

There were twelve of us, and when we could relax long enough to laugh, we called ourselves the dirty dozen. The movie stars who played in the film about World War II by the same name would have been appalled at the comparison. Their script was much more humane than ours. We were trained to utilize every method of killing and torture known to modern man.

I can't remember ever being remorseful over the death of an enemy, no matter what method was used to kill him or her. That isn't a contradiction of my earlier statement about reverence for life. When someone tries to punch your ticket, you have no alternative but to retaliate, if you value your own life. And I've never really had time to think about an enemy as being human.

Things were basic in Vietnam. It came down to staying alive. There was nothing complex about it, nothing phony. We always knew what had to be done.

Herb was the first to die, a bamboo stake from a booby trap sticking completely through his body.

But death tracked us all. Everyone in the outfit died except me. Again I had to wonder, just as I had when Roland died, why not me?"

5

From the time I first met her, Deseret has been on my mind constantly. Memories of her face, her presence, have monopolized my subconscious.

In the beginning, the vulnerability I felt, caused by a girl I really didn't know, was as disquieting as any feelings I've ever known. Her seemingly omnipresence made me think I had totally lost control of my senses.

Regarding these feelings toward her, I have since established a truce between my emotions and intellect. Intellectually, I keep telling myself she is not the most important thing in my life. Emotionally, I'm not so sure.

I'm also not sure how she feels about me. Of course, I'd like to think there is some sort of magic to our relationship, limited though it has been, but that may just be wishful thinking on my part

I've hesitated to use the word love, though it is difficult not to do so. It's just that there are so many barriers between us — the difference in our ages being one of the major obstacles. Maybe I'm more afraid of the age thing than she is, or maybe that's just what I want to think.

During the first week of the semester, I saw Deseret only in class. After each class she asked me a question of two, but that was the extent of our contact. Since she was in a class with a hundred forty-nine other students, all vying for attention, the surroundings were not the best for getting to know her.

Our first unhurried contact came on a warm and humid night during the second week of the semester.

My apartment is on the south side of Central Expressway and fairly close to Old Town, a large cluster of shops, restaurants and so on with a contrived English village ambiance. I can't say whether Old Town has or hasn't achieved the atmosphere intended by its founders. But I don't guess it matters one way or the other since business thrives in the area, especially the bars and restaurants that cater to the college crowd.

Anyway, when the spirit moves me to do a little jogging, my usual three-mile course takes me adjacent to Old Town. So, I was huffing and puffing in this vicinity when a blue Jaguar pulled up alongside me and a female voice said, "You look like you could use a ride."

It was Deseret.

I stopped, came over and leaned on the roof of the car and replied, "That bad, huh?" I could feel the air-conditioned coolness inside the car rushing out her opened window.

She laughed. "Well, you do look like you're in pain."

"In this case, looks aren't deceiving," I replied with a smile.

Some people jog for health reasons, others because they want to be seen in their designer jogging outfits. I'm an incognito jogger. I wear old gray sweats and jog only after dark. And because I consider jogging a mindless exercise, I do it only when I'm angry at myself.

On this occasion, I was angry at myself for eating too much Blue Bell ice cream after dinner. This fantastic tasting ice cream is made by a creamery at Brenham, Texas, and when a gallon of it is in the freezer compartment of my refrigerator, my mind will not let me rest until I've eaten it all.

Unaware of all this, Deseret said, "Why don't you hop in and I'll drive us over to Swensen's and buy you a banana split."

Swensen's is an ice cream parlor in Old Town.

"I'd better not get in your car," I replied, "because my clothes are wet with perspiration and a bit smelly."

"Oh, don't be silly. You just smell manly, and these are leather seats. You're not going to hurt them."

I suppose I should have confessed that I was already suffering from an overdose of ice cream, but the opportunity to know her better caused me to keep my lips sealed. I got in the car and she quickly herded it through traffic.

When seated inside Swenson's, I said, "I'd offer to buy, but all I'm carrying is the key to my apartment."

She took on a mischievious look. "Are you offering me the key for a banana split?"

It was my turn to be amused. "Hardly. Not unless you want to go over and clean the place."

"I not only don't do windows, I don't do housework."

"Whatever happened to those good old-fashioned girls?" I asked.

"I don't know," she answered, "but none of them go to SMU."

When the waitress came, we both ordered banana splits. I ordered mine without chocolate ice cream or syrup.

"You don't like chocolate?"

"Can't stand it," I said. "I'm a vanilla type of guy. Of course, I like fresh strawberries, peaches or bananas in my ice cream."

"I'd die without chocolate."

"I certainly don't want you to be without chocolate, then, because I don't want you dying."

"Speaking of dying, wasn't it awful about the dean?"

"Sure was."

"Do you know what I heard?"

I laughed. "I dunno, maybe."

She smiled. "Very funny. Anyway, I heard you had been asked to look into the dean's death."

"Now, who would tell you something like that?"

"It's all over the campus."

"A few faculty members asked me to see what I could find out from the police."

"Why would they ask you?"

"I have no idea."

She was seemingly amused by my response. "Of course you don't."

"I don't."

The waitress brought our banana splits, which looked and were delicious. However, the dessert was no competition for Deseret. In a yellow shorts outfit that accentuated her beautiful and perfectly tanned legs, she was uppermost in my mind. She had all my attention.

"Do you know what they say about you?" she asked.

"The reason why you were asked to look into the dean's death?"

"I have no idea. I don't even know who *they* are."

"Students and faculty members," she said. "They say you were with the CIA."

I laughed. "They do, huh?"

"Well, were you?"

"People just like to talk."

"That doesn't answer my question."

"Even if I had been a CIA operative, that wouldn't necessarily qualify me to investigate a murder."

"Oh, you do think it was a murder then?"

"The police have ruled it a suicide."

"Everyone on campus says you think it was murder."

"It's just a gut feeling with me," I said. "I just don't think the dean was the type to commit suicide. But I could be wrong. Hell, it wouldn't be the first time."

"You know what I'd like to do?"

"What?"

"I'd like to help you investigate the murder."

Her statement surprised me. "As much as I appreciate your offer, there's not going to be much of an investigation. I'm just going to check with the police regarding their findings."

"It could be my class project," she said.

"Your what?"

"You know, you said we all had to have a class project."

I showed my amusement. "That's right, but you're in a public relations class. I can't see how a murder investigation would qualify as a PR project. That is," I added, "if there was going to be a murder investigation."

She went into a mock pout. "You just don't want me around."

"Quite the contrary, but I'm a professor, not a detective."

"But you know quite a bit about that sort of thing."

"No, some people *think* I know quite a bit about it."

She gave me an amused look. "Sure, you're just the naive professor."

Her look and comment caused me to chuckle. "I wish I did know as much as I get credit for knowing, but let's get away from the morbid. I'd like to know more about you."

"If I tell you all about me, will you tell me all about you?" she teased.

"Since I'm so much older than you, I've got a whole lot more to tell."

"You're not that much older."

"I wish."

"I'm afraid you're not going to find me very interesting," she said.

"You're wrong. I already find you interesting."

"I'll take that as a compliment."

"You should," I said. "I just can't believe I didn't see you on campus until this semester. Were you in school last spring?"

"Yes, but I live at home, and I didn't spend much time on campus last fall or spring. In fact, I've been enrolled at SMU for the past couple of years. Until this year though, I just came to class and left as soon as a class was over."

"But you're more involved this year?"

"Oh yes, the sorority and all."

"Do you work?"

"Hardly," she said with a laugh. "My parents just want me to be involved. They don't want me underfoot all the time."

"What does your dad do?"

"He owns an accounting firm."

"I assume he does pretty well, if it's his car you're driving."

"That's not his car, it's mine," she said.

"Then I assume he does very well."

She laughed again. "I guess I'm a pretty lucky girl." She pushed a hand toward me, one finger of which was carrying a large diamond ring. "This is what my parents gave me for my birthday."

"Nice," I said. "I noticed the ring the other day after class, but thought maybe you were engaged."

Her eyes twinkled. "Maybe you're not a good detective. An engagement ring is worn on the left hand."

"Hey, I've already told you that I'm not a detective."

"And you're doing nothing more than a cursory investigation of the dean's death?"

"That's right."

"Well, Brian, I hope you'll forgive me for saying that you're full of it."

"There's nothing to forgive, Dez. As for me being full of it, maybe the people who told you all that stuff about me are the ones you ought to think are full of it."

"Maybe so," she agreed. "But when I think about it, I can't even believe I'm sitting here talking to one of my professors the way I'm talking to you."

"I told you I want to be accessible."

"You are. No one can deny that. I do have a confession to make, though."

"I'm no priest."

"I know, but I do think you're entitled to know that driving by where you were jogging tonight was no accident."

"What do you mean?"

"Some of the other students told me you jog at night, and where, so I just took a chance. I was waiting on you."

"I'm an occasional jogger, not a serious one. This just happens to be one of the nights I decided to get some exercise. But you can talk to me anytime. Why did you feel it necessary to talk to me tonight?"

She turned somber. "With all the other students around, I feel uncomfortable talking to you at school."

"I don't know if you noticed," I said. "but there are a few students in here."

"Yes, I noticed. And tomorrow it will be all over campus that we had a banana split together."

"Does that bother you?" I asked.

"No, does it bother you?"

"I'm not sure. Why did you feel it necessary to see me tonight? Was it because you wanted to join me on this so-called murder investigation?"

"Partly," she said. "It's not the kind of thing I wanted to discuss with you where other people could overhear me."

I guess maybe I wanted her to say she just wanted to be with me. But I didn't want to prompt her. "Look, Dez, this thing with the dean isn't something to play with, whether it's suicide or murder. I feel a bit uncomfortable even discussing it, because I'm really ignorant about a lot of the stuff the police uncovered."

She didn't reply immediately, then said, "I hope I wasn't flippant about wanting to help."

"Oh no," I assured. "It's just something I don't know a lot about. And it really isn't something that would qualify as a public relations project."

My response caused her to smile. "I don't guess it does," she said. "Actually, you don't like teaching public relations anyway, do you?"

"Is it that obvious?" I replied with a chuckle. "No, I prefer my magazine writing and advanced reporting classes."

"Would that advanced reporting be investigative reporting?"

We laughed together. We talked for quite awhile about nothing in particular, then she said, "It's getting late. Can I give you a lift home?"

"After all that ice cream, I'd better jog," I said.

6

Though I did not tell Deseret, I had already talked to the police regarding the dean's alleged suicide. I had, as anticipated, received the standard police line reserved for outsiders. Police take a dim view of anyone investigating one of their investigations. I did not expect them to welcome my intrusion with open arms, and I was not disappointed.

Which brings us up to date.

Seeking evidence as to whether the dean was murdered or committed suicide is difficult when I am so preoccupied with thoughts of Deseret. I now fear that my rejection of her offer to aid me in the investigation might create an uncrossable chasm between us. Of course, if she is so easily dissuaded, so be it. Circumstances being what they are, it is impossible for me to engage in pursuit of her, unless I am first assured that she desires my attention.

I'm not sure I can live with the aforementioned, but I will try.

"What have you found out, ace?" The question came from Dave McPherson, and while I was trying to choke down some fried chicken livers, Jell-o and tossed salad at a cafeteria across the street from our offices.

"Nothing," I replied.

"Nothing," he said. "From anybody I get nothing. From you I expect results."

"Kiss it, pal. I don't have time for your crap."

Dave was eating some sort of macaroni and beef mixture that made the chicken livers look good.

"Hey, don't be so testy," he said. "As short as you are on friends, you don't want to alienate the only one you have on campus."

I snorted. "Yeah, you're right. Now that the dean's gone, there's only the chairman and you who will stand up for me."

Dave was wearing starched and pressed jeans and a blue denim shirt. He hasn't worn a tie in years. He doesn't have much hair on his head, but plenty on his face. He hasn't shaved in years, either.

"Really, what have you found out so far?" he asked.

I sighed. "The police haven't been very helpful, but I expected that. I've made a few inquiries and found that the dean didn't have any money or woman problems. Of course, he may have had a man problem."

Dave laughed. "You're not out to prove he was queer, are you?"

"You were closer to him than I was," I teased. "Seriously, everything I've uncovered so far points to a man who had a lot to live for. I would like to go through his house, all his personal effects."

"I don't know who you'd see to get permission to do that."

"I don't intend to see anyone," I said.

Dave rolled his eyes. "Oh, boy. I don't know what you expect to find, though. The police have already looked through the place."

"The difference is that they were looking through the home of a suicide victim. I'll be checking out the home of a murdered man."

"Yeah, I can see where that would make a difference in one's perspective."

"I also need to go through his office, but I doubt that I'd get much cooperation from his secretary in that regard."

"I doubt that you'll get any," Dave said.

"Well, I'll just have to do my checking at night when no one is there."

"For gosh sakes, don't get caught."

"Why, are you afraid I'll involve you and your cohorts in this mess. Just remember that you're the one who got me into it in the first place."

"You're the one who said it wasn't a suicide." He was being defensive.

"Yeah, but I didn't care one way or the other."

"Don't give me that line of crap. I know how that weird mind of yours works. If we hadn't asked you to check, you'd have done it anyway."

Dave's assessment might be correct, though of late my mind has been a bit muddled.

He changed the subject with, "Why don't you and Janice come over to the house for dinner Saturday night?"

The reference was to Janice Fuller, a pretty English professor who I dated occasionally. She is thirty-two.

Betty, Dave's wife, played cupid by introducing us.

"Have you cleared this with Betty?" I asked.

Dave acted surprised by the question. "Of course. Betty's been wanting to see you. And you know she likes Janice."

"Janice is okay."

"Just okay?"

"Well, she's not someone I want to wake up with every morning. But then, I can't think of anyone who fits that category right now."

It was a lie, but caution is often my ally.

"Are you going to come over or not?"

"I'll check with Janice and let you know. But am I welcome if I just arrive alone?"

"You know you are."

After taking care of an afternoon class, I accepted an invitation to join a few students for happy hour at Mariano's, a Mexican restaurant in Old Town. I've found that these informal sessions with students often provide better opportunities for teaching than a classroom setting. Maybe it's because the students are more relaxed. But then, so am I.

Anyway, after a couple of drinks with the students I went to my apartment, took a swim in the complex's pool, worked on lesson plans and prepared dinner. This is a habitual weekday schedule for me, broken somewhat by colder weather when the swimming pool is closed.

My plan was to examine the late dean's home between nine and ten o'clock. Just as I was about to leave my apartment, the doorbell rang. I answered it to find Deseret standing there, holding a sack in one hand.

"What in the —"

She interrupted by pushing the sack toward me and saying, "Blueberry sundaes. Are you going to invite me in?"

"Sure," I said, opening the door wider and taking the sack. "This is somewhat of a surprise, though."

"Since you're not a chocolate person, I hope you like blueberries."

"I like them, but you shouldn't have gone to the trouble."

"It was no trouble. But they're going to melt if we don't eat them pretty fast."

We seated ourselves at the dining table just off the kitchen and started eating the sundaes.

"I'm really curious as to how you knew where I lived."

"It's no great secret," she said. "Everyone knows where you live."

I laughed. 'That's a bit of an exaggeration isn't it?"

"You know what I mean. I'm talking about a lot of the students at the university."

"Yeah, I know what you mean." I smiled at her. "If I had known you were coming by, I would have cleaned up the place."

"It looks fine to me, but I probably shouldn't have come unannounced. You could have been entertaining one of your female friends."

It was obvious she was fishing. I didn't take the bait. "What surprises me is that a beautiful girl like you isn't being entertained by some young man tonight."

"Young men don't interest me."

"You just haven't met the right one."

She signed. "I guess not. Listen, I don't want to keep you from doing whatever you need to do tonight."

"Oh, I wasn't going to do anything in particular."

"You were going out?"

"I just had a couple of errands to run." I had learned late in the afternoon that Reginald's sister would be in town the next day to begin moving his personal effects from his house and office. She was going to put the house on the market. That meant I had to make my move immediately.

"Well, I can't stay long anyway," Deseret said. "I've got homework to do."

"You shouldn't take classes that require homework," I said teasingly.

"It's for your class," she replied.

I smiled. "That's different."

After a flurry of small talk, she got up to leave and said, "I hope I didn't make you uncomfortable, coming by here and all. I don't know whether other students have dropped in on you like this or not."

"To tell the truth, not very many people, students or otherwise, drop in on me. Some weekends I play a little touch football or basketball with some of the guys, and afterward they come by for a beer. But you're the first female student who has been in here."

"But not the first female?"

I ignored her questioning statement and said, "The blueberry sundae was good. The company was even better."

She was pleased by the response. "Well, thank you."

After she left, I drove to and parked in a shopping area

near Reginald's house. From there I jogged to my destination, which is a small but expensive older home in Highland Park. One of the primary reasons why land — and houses — are so expensive in Highland Park is because this municipality located within the city limits of Dallas has been successful in keeping minorities out. Of course, there are a lot of great liberals in Highland Park, but their concern for mankind takes a back seat to concern for property values.

Highland Park is one of those areas where jogging is fashionable, but where it's not cool to pay any attention to what anyone else is doing. Therefore, I figured jogging attire was a good cover for what I was going to do. Of course, no one in Highland Park would dare jog wearing anything other than a designer outfit, but I was operating under cover of darkness. And plain old sweats can pass for a designer outfit in the dark. In the daylight, too, for that matter.

It probably took me all of five seconds to open the locked front door of Reginald's house. Since I had been in the house previously for a faculty function, I already knew there was no burglar alarm. Burglars are not allowed in Highland Park, so there was no need for an alarm.

My miniature flashlight provided ample illumination. A quick check of the living room revealed nothing out of the ordinary. There was no hidden wall safe, nothing in or under the couch cushions and chairs, nothing taped to the bottom of tables or behind the pictures hanging on the walls. There were no loose bricks in the fireplace to provide evidence of a hidden compartment.

Of course, I had anticipated finding little, if anything, in the house. However, I did figure any clues I might find would be in Reginald's personal papers, either at his home or university office. He used one of his three bedrooms as a home office.

In that bedroom was a large desk, filing cabinets, and the usual office paraphernalia. It was a small room, so the oversized furniture, including a leather desk chair and recliner, seemed out of place. The first thing I noticed on the desk was the framed portrait of a woman, who I already knew was Reginald's ex-wife. It was the same picture that occupied space on his desk at the university.

I was busily engaged in checking out the contents of the desk drawers when I heard something. Someone else was in the house.

My immediate concern was that someone had seen me enter and had called the police. My mind quickly dismissed that theory because the police would simply have covered all exits from the house and called for my surrender. Whoever this intruder was, he was exercising extreme stealth. Therefore, I killed my light and took a position where I could surprise him.

When the shadowy figure entered the room, I immediately sprang from my position and crashed into him, pushing him forward onto the floor and locking a forearm around his neck. I would have rendered him unconscious except for the barely audible female shriek exclaiming, "For god's sake, you're killing me."

It was Deseret.

I turned her over on her back and asked, "What in the hell are you doing here?"

Even in the darkness, I was aware of her smile. "I could ask you the same thing," she said.

Since I had been discovered, there was no point in trying to answer, nor to even try to come up with a logical explanation.

"Did I hurt you?"

"I've had gentler treatment," she replied.

"You're lucky I didn't break your neck."

"I'll say."

"Dez, I'll ask again. What in the world are you doing here?"

"I followed you. I thought you said you weren't going to look into the dean's murder?"

"All right, so I'm looking into it. Or maybe I'm the murderer, in which case you're in an awful lot of trouble."

"No, you're not the murderer," she said. "And I don't see how you can keep me from helping you now."

"It'll be easy," I replied. "You don't need to be involved in this mess, so I just won't let you be."

"One of the nice things about having me involved is that I'll have to keep my mouth shut. I'll be guilty of breaking and entering, too."

I sighed. "Blackmail, huh? Oh, hell, as long as you're here you can keep me company."

"Believe it or not, I might even be able to help you."

"I don't even know what I'm looking for."

"Well, I'll check the filing cabinets while you're checking the desk," she said.

"Okay, just look for anything that seems unusual for a college administrator."

Luckily, I had brought an extra flashlight, a carryover

from the old days when I insisted on a backup for every piece of essential equipment. There were times when such planning had meant the difference between life and death.

We had been going through Reginald's papers for about fifteen minutes or so when figures on some of his bank records sent up a warning signal.

"Whoa," I said. "For a college administrator, ol' Reg was in very good financial shape."

"Maybe he inherited some money," Deseret suggested.

"Maybe, but what I'm seeing here leads me to believe the man was a millionaire. And he didn't get to be one on his pay from the university."

"He has a lot of property, too," Deseret said, handing me a thick file containing legal documents. "These are copies. He must have the originals in a safety deposit box."

"Along with stocks and bonds," I replied. "There's a copy of a report from his stockbroker here that's quite impressive."

With my handy little government issue camera, I photographed the papers and records I found interesting. I also found a sheet of paper with nothing but numbers on it. I thought I knew what they represented, but would have to run a check.

In the desk was a small black book with names, phone numbers and what I interpreted as some sort of code after each name. I just took the book, figured the sister wouldn't know about it anyway.

"Let's get out of here," I said.

"Do you have everything you need?"

"Enough."

Outside the house and walking toward our cars, Deseret asked, "Where to now?"

"I think it might be wise for you to go home," I said.

"Why, aren't you going to check his office at the university now?"

I shook my head in resignation and said, "Don't press it, Dez."

"But that is what you're going to do, isn't it?"

I didn't respond.

When we arrived at her car, I opened the door for her. Before getting in she turned to say something to me, but before any words could exit her mouth I pulled her into my arms and pressed my lips against hers. It was a long, tender kiss.

"I didn't expect that," she said.

"Neither did I. Now go home and I'll see you tomorrow."

Surprisingly, she didn't argue.

When she drove away, I knew she would go home. As for me, I still had work to do. I had to go the university and check out Reginald's office.

7

A search of Reginald's office revealed nothing of any consequence, certainly nothing to suggest that he had been murdered. However, what Deseret and I had discovered in his house had been more than enough to pique my curiosity.

"Do you know anything yet?" Dave asked while we were having coffee at the Student Union Building.

"I haven't even talked to her."

"What in the hell are you talking about?"

"I was talking about asking Janice to come with me to your house for dinner Saturday night. What in the hell are you talking about?"

"You know damn well I was talking about the suicide, murder, whatever."

I laughed. "Hey, I'm not a mind reader."

"You can be a bit exasperating," Dave said, "do you know that?"

"I've heard."

"Well, are you going to tell me what you've learned or not?"

"On one condition."

"What's that?"

"That you don't go blabbing it all over campus."

"Now, why would you say something like that?"

"Your mouth got me into this mess in the first place."

It was Dave's turn to laugh. "My lips are sealed. You have my solemn promise."

"Knowing you as I do, I'm not sure that's enough," I said. "But what the hell. Of course, some of what I'm going to tell you is pure speculation on my part."

"Hmmm. Almost everything you say or do is speculative."

"I'll ignore that. My guess, though, is that Reginald was mixed up in some sort of drug ring."

Dave's eyes took on a bewildered look, then he snorted. "You've got to be kidding."

"Hey, I'm just telling you what I think. If you don't want my opinion, just say so."

"I want your opinion," Dave assured. "If I'm amused, it's because I have difficulty believing a wimp like Reginald could be part of a drug ring."

"Okay, tell me what you think Reginald's salary was."

"Oh, I'd guess sixty to seventy thousand a year."

"Beats the hell out of what we make, doesn't it?"

"Almost anything would beat the hell out of what we make."

"What if I told you that Reginald's personal papers indicate an estate in the millions, plus some Swiss bank accounts?"

Dave showed his surprise. "That's hard to believe. Of course, he may have inherited some money."

"I've already done a little checking this morning. His folks were strictly middle-class, and he didn't inherit any money from relatives or friends, either."

"How do you find out that kind of stuff?"

"I have some sources."

"Yeah, I'll bet," Dave responded knowingly.

"Did you know Reginald was in Vietnam?" I asked.

"No, I didn't."

"He didn't see any action," I said. "He was on the headquarters staff of colonel, a real clown in an unfunny sense."

"Sounds like you knew the colonel."

"I knew him," I replied with disdain. "He was one of those guys who made a profit from the war."

"How did he do that?"

"Drugs."

"I surmise you think that's where Reginald got his start?"

"That would be my guess."

Dave grunted. "My guess is that it's more than a guess."

I smiled. "The way it reads is that Reg goes into the Army as a second lieutenant, but we both know he had the propensity for putting his nose in the right places. In a very short time he rises to the rank of captain. When he goes into the Army he's fresh from a teaching assignment and doesn't have the proverbial pot to pee in. But while in the Army, Reg builds quite a nest egg.

"When he gets out, he goes back to teaching and through shrewd investments keeps stockpiling money. And, of course, education is one of the best covers going."

"Sounds like Reg learned a lot from the colonel," Dave said.

"Chances are he was still learning from him when he met his demise."

"You mean the colonel's still operating?"

"Like a self-winding clock."

"What's this colonel's name?"

"Foster Cerney."

"Does he live here in Dallas?"

"Believe it or not, he lives near Idabel, Oklahoma." Idabel is a small southeastern Okie town.

"What's he doing up there?"

"Probably the same thing he did in Vietnam."

"A drug operation? You can't be serious!"

"Why? Do you think Idabel's too small for a major drug operation?"

"The thought occurs to me," Dave said.

"Well, that makes it an even more perfect cover. Believe me, wherever Cerney is operating, he's dirty."

"Sounds like you're not one of this guy's biggest fans."

"I can't help detesting the son of a bitch," I said. "A lot of our boys bought the farm because they were too doped up to know what they were doing."

Dave snorted. "We had a few doped up in this country, too. They did their part in keeping us from winning the war, and even from having that so-called peace with honor. But what's this got to do with Reginald?"

"My guess is that Cerney used Reginald in Vietnam and was still using him here," I replied. "Of course, I'm sure ol' Reg wanted to be used. Once you start getting all those big bucks for pushing a little dope, it's probably hard to stop."

"And you think Cerney may be the one who took Reg

out?"

"Maybe, but it could have been any number of people. When you're in the dope business, you're not dealing with the members of a church choir."

"If you knew about Cerney in Vietnam, someone in authority must have known, too."

I chuckled. "Are you saying I didn't have any authority?"

"Knowing your aversion to dope, I'd have to say you probably didn't. If you had, you'd have closed Cerney down."

"I'd have done that and more," I agreed.

I had tried to put it out of my mind, but the Colonel Foster Cerney file was one I hadn't wanted to close. Now through some quirk of fate, it had again been opened for me. My major problem in investigating Cerney was my lack of objectivity. I figured hanging was too nice a death for the man.

"Tell me more about it," Dave said.

Suddenly, I was verbalizing it, all the hatred felt for Cerney over the years.

In Vietnam, Cerney had been the epitome of an opportunist. He had teamed with South Vietnamese gangsters to sell dope to American servicemen. And, from what I was able to ascertain, had also pipelined his poison into the U.S. As to why he hadn't been stopped, he was paying the right American military and government officials.

The bitterness I felt for Cerney and his kind was forever with me. No amount of time or good things in life could ever erase the memories of young men dying and Cerney profiting.

"Are you telling me that some of our high ranking officers and government personnel were on the take?" Dave asked.

"Not just on the take," I replied, "some of them were actually responsible for major dope shipments into this country. They were also the powers that be for selling the stuff in Vietnam. Granted, there was no shortage of dope available when we went over to allegedly rescue the country from communism, but our people put the little dealers out of business and set up a corporate structure. Colonel Foster Cerney was just part of it. He was little. There was some real top brass involved."

"And Reginald?"

"A small fish, but Cerney's Number One boy at one time."

"Surely you didn't know that when you were in 'Nam."

"No, I was totally unaware of Reginald, which is understandable. Most of my time there was spent beyond what was considered the front lines. All of his was spent in the rear and, of course, in Cerney's shadow. But my source, who was one of those investigating the situation, told me about Reginald's involvement."

"Funny, I didn't even know Reginald had been in the service, much less being in Vietnam," Dave said.

"I doubt that he wanted to broadcast his part in the war," I said.

"If what you say is true, that's understandable."

"It's true. Some brass and some politicians were responsible for a lot of body bags being filled with Americans."

"Surely someone could have done something," Dave argued. "Everyone couldn't have been in on it."

"I hope I didn't imply that. There were plenty of good officers in 'Nam, but they were in the field trying to do something. As in all wars, while they were busting their butts, the rear echelon boys were lapping up the gravy."

"Still, it doesn't make sense. You knew about Cerney. Others had to know."

"Obviously, but when you talk about making sense, you're talking about something totally alien to war. None of it made sense, but you deal with so much hearsay, rumor and red tape that it's partically impossible to get anything done.

"For instance, there might be a thousand Russian surface-to-air missiles lined up on an airfield in North Vietnam, but our planes weren't allowed to attack and destroy them. We were forced to wait until they were deployed so we could take them on one by one. That's the reason so many of our planes were shot down. So, don't talk to me about making sense."

Dave pondered the outburst, then said, "I guess there are things that many of us will never understand."

"There are things none of us will ever understand. But hell, Dave, higher authority was made aware of Cerney's activities. In the chain of command, though, he had too many friends to ever be nailed."

"Are you going to give the police what you've got?"

"I told you, some of what I've got is speculation, and the police aren't into that. They're satisfied to leave Reginald's file closed as a suicide."

Dave's expression was one of dejection. "What you're

saying is that even if Cerney was responsible for Reginald's death, nothing's going to be done about it. The man's going to be allowed to go on doing just what he did in Vietnam."

"Something's going to be done," I promised, "but not just because he might have been responsible for Reginald's death. Reginald's death isn't something that caused me to lose any sleep. I do want Cerney. I want him bad, and now he's where I can get him."

When Dave and his group has asked me to look into Reginald's death, I had halfheartedly agreed to do so. With the discovery of Foster Cerney's possible involvement, though, it was not a whole new ball game.

In discussing Cerney with Dave, I hadn't been completely honest regarding my knowledge of the man's activities in Vietnam. The truth is, very late in the game Cerney became one of my projects, about two months before the U.S. forces pulled out of the country. My source told me the reason I hadn't run into Reginald during my brief investigation was because he had left Vietnam several months earlier.

My investigation of Cerney had been very hampered by all the confusion associated with our withdrawal. Though I had considered him unfinished business, the Agency had not allowed me to pursue the project once he was on American soil. Now there was at least a possibility I could do it on my own.

Dave left to teach a class, I had another cup of coffee and then started across campus en route to my office. Deseret ambushed me as I was coming around a corner of the building.

substantiate such a possibility. Contrary to what Dave might say, they're the experts, not me. If they're satisfied Reginald's death was a suicide, then I have to be satisfied."

Becker nodded affirmatively. "Well, I think it was worth checking into, and we're all appreciative of your efforts."

"I didn't do all that much, Frank, just checked with the police. I'm satisfied with their conclusions, hope the rest of the faculty is, too."

"Oh, yeah, we're all satisfied," he assured. "It was just a long shot anyway."

Shamelessly, I said piously, "It was worth checking. The faculty's concern regarding Reginald's death was most touching. of course, you were much closer to him than most of us."

I couldn't believe he would buy my act, but he was so into himself that he said, "Yes, the entire faculty respected Reginald. He'll be missed."

Hopefully, Becker wasn't including me in the group who respected Reginald, nor among those who would miss him.

Eleven-thirty was soon on me and Deseret appeared in the doorway, bright-eyed and anxious. The contrast between us is quite pronounced, her being a bit hyper and me being more laid-back.

"Any particular place you'd like to go?" I asked.

"You name it."

I chose Friday's, a restaurant on Greenville Avenue. It is a particular favorite of many students, though I don't share their enthusiasm. It's too noisy. However, it was a balmy day and the restaurant has tables outside. That's where we chose to sit.

Deseret ordered a glass of white wine as a prelude to the meal. It was too early for me. I opted for ice tea.

"You know I'm going to ask you if you found anything in the dean's office," she said.

"I didn't find anything."

"I'm not sure you'd tell me if you did."

"I'm not sure I would, either."

"Don't be difficult, Brian. I can be a big help to you."

"Help on what?"

"The murder investigation."

"It's over. I've done all I can."

"I don't believe that."

For some reason I didn't find her persistence annoying, so I chuckled and said, "What you believe or don't believe is immaterial, Dez. There's nothing else I can do."

"So, what are your conclusions?"

"Oh, I think he was murdered, but if the police choose to rule it a suicide there's nothing I can do. By the way, I'd appreciate it if you'd keep what I think confidential."

"About him being murdered you mean?"

"Yeah," I said. "That's not what I told the journalism chairman. The only other person on campus who knows what I think is Dave McPherson."

"I'm not going to say anything. I figured you'd tell Professor McPherson. He's your best friend, isn't he?"

"Yeah, he is." Then on impulse I continued, "What are you doing Saturday night?"

She smiled. "It depends on what you have in mind."

"I'm having dinner at the McPhersons, thought you

might like to join me."

"I'd love to."

Betty, I figured, wouldn't be too pleased with my dinner date, since she had been trying to pair me permanently with Janice Fuller. Maybe Deseret's appearance on the scene would at least slow down Betty's cupid tendencies.

"What shall I wear?" Deseret asked.

"It will be very casual," I said. "Dave will probably just cook some steaks on an outdoor grill. If it's cool enough, we'll probably eat outside."

"Do you want to pick me up at my house?"

"I will, but I don't relish the idea of meeting your parents," I said. "What will they think of me? Too old for you?"

She looked amused. "I don't know. They're in their fifties, and you're only thirty-nine."

"And you're only nineteen."

"I'm twenty," she said defensively.

"Excuse me."

"I need another glass of wine."

After signaling the waiter and giving him her order, I said, "You'd better watch that stuff. Don't you have any classes this afternoon?"

"You're driving, and no, I don't have any classes this afternoon. Would you like to do anything?"

"You're impossible, do you know that? I do have some work to do."

"Don't get in a huff. I just thought if you didn't have anything to do, we could spend the afternoon together."

"Doing what?"

"I don't know. I'm open to suggestions."

I shook my head in mock dismay. Fortunately, the food arrived and we busied ourselves with eating, and with meaningless conversation like, "Good, isn't it?" and "It's sure a nice day."

Such small talk might seem boring to some, but I was really tired of playing defense. I like to think that I started playing offense when I said, "One of the things I want to do this afternoon is talk to the dean's sister. You can tag along if you like."

The invitation surprised her. "I'd like that. I'd like it very much."

I knew Reginald's sister was at his house, packing everything and getting it ready for the movers. We drove to the house, rang the doorbell, and were greeted by a tall, attractive woman who I guessed to be in her early forties. If she looked like Reginald in any way, it was hidden from me.

After we introduced ourselves, she told us her name was Julia Wood and invited us in.

"I'm sorry for the intrusion," I said, "but we just wanted to come by and convey our sympathies."

"Thank you," she replied. "Your thoughtfulness is appreciated, and I welcome an interruption from the drudgery of all this packing."

"I would have expressed my sympathy to you at the funeral, but unfortunately was unable to attend," I lied.

"Well, it's nice of you to do so now, and it really wasn't necessary. So many people came up to me at the funeral that I really don't remember any of them. Except, of course, Frank Becker."

"Reg and Frank were very close," I said. "Had you met Frank previously?"

She hesitated in responding, then said, "No, the funeral was the first time. But enough talk about the funeral. I've just made some coffee. Would either of you like some?"

Both of us accepted her invitation, so she led us back to the kitchen where we filled our cups and doctored the black liquid. Then the three of us seated ourselves at a small breakfast table.

"I realize Reg's death may be difficult for you to talk about," I said, "but can you think of any reason why he would commit suicide?"

She pondered the question, then replied, "I have no idea. Maybe he was depressed about money, and I know he was depressed about his divorce."

My surprise was obvious. "His divorce? Hadn't he been divorced for about ten years?"

She quickly responded, "A long period of time doesn't necessarily heal the hurt."

She was right, of course. And Reginald did keep pictures of his ex-wife on his desk at both office and home. I wasn't, however, buying remorse over an ill-fated marriage as a reason for suicide. Nor was I buying financial problems. Julia Wood had to know of her brother's wealth, so even her mention of possible money problems, no matter how innocent the remark, caused suspicion on my part.

"You wouldn't have any reason to believe it wasn't suicide, would you?"

Now it was her turn to be suspicious. "What do you mean by that?" she asked. "Why would you even think it was something other than suicide?"

"I don't mean anything by it," I said. "It's just hard for me to believe that Reg would kill himself. He didn't seem the type."

There was an awkward silence, then she said, "I don't know what the type is, but Reginald was never a happy boy or man. If you were a close friend, you'd probably know that."

"We weren't that close. I guess he was closer to Franklin Becker than to anyone else on the faculty." As an afterthought I added, "Did he ever mention a Foster Cerney to you?"

Her eyes flashed recognition at the name, but she quickly replied, "The name doesn't ring a bell."

Eyes are funny things. During our conversation, until I asked the question about Cerney, we had maintained eye contact. Now her eyes were furtive, and I sensed that nervousness had overwhelmed her previously calm demeanor. Though she was cordial enough, her body language suggested she was ready for us to go.

As we were leaving, she commented, "Professor Stratford, I'm sure you've been through my brother's house before, haven't you?"

It was more than a question. Her eyes were more interested in reading my face than her ears were interested in my response.

"I've been here a few times," I said, wondering if she suspected I'd gone through Reginald's papers. Maybe she even knew about the book I had taken. "Why do you ask?"

"If you're familiar with the house, I thought maybe

you'd know someone who might want to buy it."

Her answer was a lie, but I said matter-of-factly, "You won't have any trouble selling a house in Highland Park."

After we were in the car, Deseret said, "That woman is a phony."

I laughed. "Well, I don't know about that, but she is a liar."

"You mean about knowing Foster Cerney?"

"You picked up on that, huh?"

"It was pretty easy to do. Who is Foster Cerney?"

I started to tell her he was no one of any consequence, then decided what the hell. I told her the whole story.

When I had finished, she said, "You're going after him, of course."

"It's one of those things I have to do."

"I'd like to help."

"I appreciate it, but Cerney's much too dangerous. I wouldn't feel comfortable if you were involved."

My response caused her to be strangely subdued, and silent. "Are you okay?" I asked.

She faked a smile and said, "I'm fine. Would you mind dropping me at my car?"

Her shift in mood bothered me, but I'm hardly justified in complaining about the moodiness of others. My own mood changes are as unpredictable as the Texas weather. So, I left Deseret at her car and went to my office.

It took several calls, but I finally got an address and phone number for Reginald's ex-wife. She had been remarried for several years and was living in Atlanta. When she answered the phone, I identified myself and stated my business. She told me she hadn't even heard about Reginald's death.

"That surprises me," I said. "I assumed you still kept in touch since he had pictures of you on desks at his office and home."

"Him keeping my pictures surprises me," she replied. "We never really got along. Ours was a marriage that was doomed from the beginning."

"When was the last time you saw him?"

"Oh, I can't remember exactly, But it's probably been ten years."

"I don't guess you knew much about his business affairs?"

She laughed. "That's an understatement. I didn't know anything about our business affairs when we were married. He was always pretty secretive, which was part of the problem."

"Did you ever hear the name Foster Cerney?"

"I can't recall, but then I didn't know many of Reginald's friends or business associates. His parents were nice, though, and his sister and I kept in touch until she died."

The information stunned me. "His sister is dead? Did he have more than one?"

No, just Mrs. Julia Wood. She lived in Houston."

"When did she die?"

"About three years ago."

We talked for a few more minutes, during which time Reg's ex-wife said she couldn't accept the fact that he committed suicide.

"If he did, it wasn't because of remorse or guilt," she said. "Reginald was not a man to feel guilty about anything he did."

The conversation left me with a number of questions, the primary one being the identity of the woman posing as Reg's sister. Why hadn't she been exposed at the funeral? His sister was supposed to have been his only living relative, or course, but surely some of his friends knew the real sister was dead. Or did they?

If not, why had Reginald Masters kept his sister's death a secret?

There were reasons why I wouldn't have known. I had been at the school only two years, and I wasn't one of Reg's confidants. But what about Franklin Becker? What about Reg's secretary?

I knew it was a long shot, but I drove back to Reg's house in hopes of finding the woman who called herself Julia Wood. When no one answered the doorbell, I let myself in.

None of the furniture was missing, but every drawer in the house had been searched. And everything from Reginald's desk and file cabinets had been taken.

The dean had been involved in something big, and I was determined to find out just what.

8

The next day I asked Martha Paul, the dean's secretary, how well she knew his sister.

"I don't know her at all," she said. "The only time I ever met her was at his funeral."

I filled in with, "Which is when she told you she was going to pack and move Reg's stuff, and sell his house?" It had been Martha who had told me what day the phony sister planned to do her packing.

"That's right. Why? Is something wrong?"

"No, I was just curious," I said. I had already decided Martha probably didn't know anything. In doing some checking, I discovered she had been employed by the university just a month before me.

I continued, "I just met the sister yesterday and wondered how well you knew her."

"She seemed very nice," Martha said, "but to tell the truth, until the funeral I didn't even know the dean had a sister."

"It's kind of strange that he never mentioned her to you, isn't it?"

"He never discussed anything personal with me, and he didn't want me to discuss anything personal with him. I hate to say it, him being dead and all, but he was sort of a queer duck. He was real secretive about everything he did."

Martha was the kind of person with whom most people would have felt safe in sharing things of a personal nature. She was getting close to sixty, had four grandchildren, and had been married to the same man for almost forty years. She and her husband had known heartbreak. A granddaughter had overdosed on drugs.

"Then I don't guess you were surprised about him committing suicide?"

"I don't know about that," she said. "Something that drastic would surprise anybody."

After a cup of Martha's coffee, which wasn't bad, and a bit more conversation, I made my way to Franklin Becker's office. He was, as usual, acting very busy. He is a great paper shuffler.

Feeling such disgust for Becker, I hesitate to describe him. He truly is an almost mirror image of the late Reginald Masters. He is short, flabby, and has a nondescript face. Oh, his jowls and bulbous nose are fairly pronounced, but basically there is a softness and weakness about him that is offensive in a man.

"I can give you a few minutes, Brian, but I really have a lot of work to do."

"I won't take much of your time," I said, "I was just curious as to how well you know Reg's sister."

"Why do you ask?" There was, I surmised, suspicion in his voice. But again, I stress that I'm not exactly objective about Franklin Becker.

"No particular reason, Frank. I just met the woman

yesterday and she asked me to keep an eye out for anyone who might be interested in buying Reg's house."

The answer seemingly caused him to relax a little, to let his guard down. "Oh, I see. But you don't have to worry about finding a buyer for the house. I've bought it."

"Really? That surprises me. The house you have now is very nice."

"Well, I'm not buying it to live in," he said. "I'm buying it as an investment property."

"It ought to be a good one. I wish I could have afforded to buy it."

Becker knew what I was thinking, that there was no way he could afford two houses on a university salary, and especially a house in Highland Park.

He gave an uneasy chuckle and said, "Julia let me steal the house. I told her it was worth three times what I could pay, but she said she wanted one of Reg's friends to have it."

"She must be a very generous woman. Since you're on a first name basis, I guess you've known her for some time?"

Becker realized he had trapped himself in reference to knowing the phony Julia Wood, but he had no idea I knew the truth about Reginald's sister. Still, he showed nervousness and reluctance in his response.

"Oh, I don't know her that well," he said. "I had only met her a couple of times prior to the funeral."

"Really? That makes her generosity toward you all the more unique."

After leaving Becker's office, I went to my own with the knowledge that the chairman might very well be deeply involved in the same sinister activities in which Reginald Masters had been engaged. All my senses were operating at the "extreme caution" level.

Deseret was in my office.

When our eyes met, it was like we had suddenly stopped drifing and had begun to see for the very first time. There was a silent coming together that needed no verbal explanation.

We kissed.

We held each other close.

I think we both realized that it had begun for real and that there was no way to stop it.

Earlier I mentioned the situation that occurred in the fall. The situation was meeting Deseret. The result was what was happening now, something I had feared from the first. I was in love with her, and totally out of control in terms of directing my emotions.

She was like a prisoner in my subconscious, one that I could never free. She was also my captor, one from whom I never wantcd to escape.

9

Diner with Dave and Betty was as I anticipated. Betty was cool toward Deseret, and Dave was amused by the entire situation.

Early in the evening Betty pulled me aside and said, "My god, Brian, she's young enough to be your daughter."

"There's a few years difference between your age and Dave's, too."

"Ten isn't like twenty," she argued.

"Nineteen," I corrected.

"Whatever, it's still cradle robbing."

"You're just teed off because I didn't bring Janice."

"Maybe I am," she agreed. "Janice is a neat gal, and I'd hope you would have a lot more in common with her than with Deseret."

I laughed. "Now what does that mean?"

"You figure it out."

"Dez is a neat woman," I said with emphasis. "You'll see."

Betty is a pretty lady, smart and sophisticated. She's brought Dave's sophistication level up considerably since they married several years ago. Dave's even into making judgments on wine now, somthing that doesn't appeal to me. When I first met Dave, he was more interested in good cream gravy and biscuits than in wine.

They make quite a twosome; Dave, a picture of relaxed shagginess, in tandem with his blonde, blue-eyed and vivacious wife.

As the evening wore on, Betty warmed to Deseret. It would have been hard to do otherwise. Dez is a match for anyone in wit and charm.

Over coffee at a redwood table on the patio, Dave asked, "Does Dez know what a rogue you are?"

Deseret smiled. "Forewarned is forearmed, and I've had plenty of warnings."

"I'm not sure you know just how devious Brian is," Betty contributed.

"Whoa," I said. "You two could throw a monkey wrench into my plans for this young lady."

"I would hope she's smart enough to sabotage your plans for her," Betty said. "You wouldn't want to share any of those plans with us, would you, Brian?"

I defended myself with, "I think you two have the wrong idea about us. Dez has just been helping me investigate Reginald's death."

Both Dave and Betty gave each other furtive, surprised glances.

"I wanted to ask you if anything new had developed," Dave said, "but I wasn't sure whether or not I should say anything in front of Deseret."

"She knows everything," I said, then proceeded to bring Dave and Betty up-to-date on everything I had learned.

After pondering the information, Betty said, "If I were you, Deseret, I'd think twice about getting involved in something like this. If Brian's right, some of Reginald Masters's friends might be nasty and vicious people."

"Oh, Brian's right," was the response, "but I don't think I have anything to worry about."

"I hope you don't expect him to protect you," Dave said jokingly. "When he was allegedly in the Air Force, I spent a lot of sleepless nights knowing that he was between me and the enemy."

I shook my head in mock disgust.

"So far, he's been a little overly protective," Deseret complained.

"My plan is to have Dez do a little detail work for me," I said. "I'd just as soon no one know that she's involved in any way."

Betty laughed. "From just this brief time with Deseret, I'd say she's not going to be satisfied doing Mickey Mouse work. You've got a partner, Brian, whether you want one or not."

Since I wasn't yet ready to meet Deseret's parents, she had driven her own car to the McPhersons. Outside their house we embraced and Deseret asked, "Will you call me tomorrow?"

"What time?"

"It doesn't matter."

"It being Sunday, I figured you'd want to sleep late."
She laughed. "Are you going to sleep late?"

"Probably not. Sleeping late gives me a headache."

"What are you going to do tomorrow?"

"My immediate plans are to do my laundry."

"Why don't I just call you when I get up? That way you don't have to worry about waking me."

"Sure, that's probably best."

She smiled. "Are you sure? You being so chauvinistic, I wouldn't want to damage that male ego of yours."

I chuckled. "Hey, I'm not that bad. I don't mind if you call."

Turning more serious, she said, "I really did enjoy the evening."

"Me, too."

We kissed again, then got in our cars and drove our separate ways.

I had wanted to ask her to come to my apartment for a glass of wine, but decided against it. Maybe I didn't trust myself to now be alone with her in such surroundings. Maybe I feared her rejection if my desire for her did get out of control. Whatever the reason, I had to now convince myself it was for the best.

While even the slightest change in environment can cause bells and warning lights to go off in my brain, there was nothing subtle about what caused the red alert in my mind when approaching the front door of my apartment.

It was ajar.

A television hero might have entered the apartment and challenged an intruder, or intruders, to hand-to-hand combat. When I don't know the odds, I become extremely cautious. I retreated to the car and from its trunk got my Ruger twenty-two caliber revolver.

For some, such a small caliber pistol might seem like lightweight firepower, but it's plenty if the bullet hits a vital spot. I'm somewhat of an expert at hitting vital spots.

I took cover and waited for all of fifteen minutes. No one came out of the apartment, nor could I hear any movement inside.

When I was relatively certain there was no one inside, I entered as I had been taught — cautiously — with my gun at the ready position. A quick, systematic check convinced me that the place was void of other human life. Whoever my visitor, or visitors, my apartment was a shambles. Furniture had been overturned, the contents of drawers emptied on the floor, clothing from the closet scattered, the mattress and pillows ripped open, couch and chair cushions torn apart.

After checking the place for electronic bugs, especially the phone, I called Deseret. She has a private line, which she answered on the second ring.

"I hope I didn't wake your parents."

"They can't hear my phone," she said.

"I hate to call you this late, but I wanted to tell you not to call me tomorrow." I then told her what had happened.

"My god," she said, "what do you supposed they were looking for?"

I hadn't told her about the black book, and saw no reason to do so now.

"I have a pretty good idea, but I'll tell you about it later."

"What are you going to do?"

"I'm going to put a few things together, then check into a motel."

"We have a guest room," she said.

I laughed. "I'm sure your folks would be thrilled to

have me as a guest."

"They wouldn't mind, especially if I told them what happened to your apartment."

My mood turned somber. "Look, Dez, I don't want to endanger you or your folks. Just stay put and don't try to contact me. I'll get in touch with you as soon as I can, but I don't even want anyone to see you with me."

"I don't like that very much."

"I don't like it either, but please, just trust me."

"You know I do."

I next called Dave and Betty. He answered the phone, laughed when he heard my voice and said, "The one time Betty doesn't have a headache and you have to call."

After hearing what I had to say, though, there was no laughter. "What have you got that they want?" he asked.

"Never mind. Just take a few precautions around there, all right? It might not be all that healthy to be my friend for the time being. Steer clear of me."

"Forget it," he said. "Betty and I aren't turning our backs on you when you're in trouble."

I knew it wouldn't do any good to argue. "Do you have a gun?" I asked.

"I have a twelve-gauge shotgun."

"Load it and keep it by your bed, and make sure your doors and windows are locked. In fact, push some furniture in front of the doors. Anyone with any savvy can unlock your doors."

"Yeah," Dave agreed, "I'm sure you could."

After making sure I wasn't being followed, I checked in at a nearby Ramada Inn. Still, I planned to sleep lightly, and with my gun at my side. I was glad I had put the black book and film of Reginald's papers in my safe deposit box.

10

Deseret was worried. She was, of course, primarily concerned for Brian's safety. But there was something else, too, something she hadn't told him when he called.

She was almost certain that, after leaving the McPhersons' house, someone had followed her home. Until Brian's call, she hadn't thought much about it. She had simply figured the driver of the car following her was a jilted and jealous boyfriend. There were several she knew of who might be inclined to do a little spying. It was one of her objections to males in her own age group. They could be very immature.

When she had turned into the driveway, the car following her had continued past the house and on up the street. Once the electronically-controlled garage door closed behind her, she hadn't given any more thought to the driver of the mystery car.

Until Brian's call.

For a residence, the big two-story house that belonged to her parents was probably as fine a sanctuary as could be found in Dallas. Her father had spared no expense in the alarm system, which was monitored by a private security company. Burglar bars were on all the windows and doors, and supposedly burglar-proof locks were on all the doors. In addition, two well-trained dobermans roamed at will inside the house.

Her father was one who didn't think the house being in Highland Park exempted it from intrusions. As to whether or not her father had a gun, she didn't know. She suspected he probably did.

No matter how secure the house, Deseret thought she would feel safer with Brian. Or maybe it was just a matter of wanting to be with him. She was very worried about him, thought he might even be safer with her.

She had already been dressed for bed when Brian called, but now she couldn't sleep. Television, which normally made her drowsy late at night, did nothing to help. She decided she was hungry.

After putting on a robe and slippers, she made her way down the stairs. At the foot of the stairs she patted one of the dobermans on the head and made her way to the kitchen. The dog followed her.

She was hungry for ice cream, but there was none in the freezer compartment of the refrigerator. Normally, a desire for ice cream would have caused her to slip on some clothes, then drive to a nearby convenience store where she could buy a gallon.

Not tonight. Not after what had happened.

She was not going to play the role of an unthinking woman who stupidly puts herself in a dangerous situation. She had seen enough of those in movie and television dramas. If something happened to her, it was not going to be because she unwittingly allowed it.

Since there was no ice cream, she settled for microwave popcorn, and shared it with the dog that seemed so interested in what she was doing.

A familiar voice interrupted her thought processes, startled her momentarily. "I thought I heard someone in the kitchen."

"Sorry, mother, I didn't mean to wake you. I didn't wake daddy, too, did I?"

"No, you know from our bedroom you can't hear anything down here. I was in the den reading, fell asleep on the couch."

Deseret considered her mother to be one of the most beautiful, most intelligent women she knew. Deseret's impression of Honey Antares was shared by almost everyone who knew her. Though fifty-one, she could easily have passed for a woman in her late thirties. She was tall and statuesque, with auburn hair that showed very little silver, and her goddess-like face was void of lines and wrinkles, though she had never submitted to cosmetic surgery.

"Do you want some popcorn?"

"No thanks. I think I'll make some coffee."

"Won't it keep you awake?"

"It doesn't affect me that way. Besides, I'm going to have decaffeinated."

"Did you know we don't have any ice cream?"

Honey laughed. "Do you think you can manage until tomorrow without going into withdrawal?"

Deseret smiled, patted herself on a thigh and said, "I probably should do without it from now on."

"You're anything but fat, Deseret. In fact, I think you

could probably use a few pounds."

Deseret sighed. "It's where I get the pounds that bothers me."

After Honey had the coffeepot going, she asked, "How was your evening?"

"It was fine."

"Just fine? Didn't you and your date have dinner with that professor and his wife?"

"Yes."

"Well, how was your date? You did go out with that professor you've talked so much about lately, didn't you?"

"How did you know?"

Honey chuckled. "If you could hear yourself rave about him to your father and me, then you'd understand. Besides, I know my daughter pretty well."

Deseret smiled. "Pretty transparent, huh?"

"Very."

"The evening was nice, but I would have preferred to have had Brian to myself."

"You didn't like his friends?"

"They're neat people, but I think Mrs. McPherson resents me a little. At least, I think she did at first."

"Why would she resent you?"

"My guess is that she thinks I'm too young for Brian, and I think she also had someone else picked out for him."

"There's nothing worse than a cupid spurned," Honey said. "As for you being too young for this Brian, maybe she's right. How old is he?"

Deseret took on that defiant look with which Honey

was well acquainted. "I'm not saying. I'll let you guess when you meet him."

"That simply means he looks younger than he is, which will probably be reason enough for me to get a few more silver hairs."

"Age isn't important," Deseret argued.

Honey poured herself a cup of coffee, then said, "It's never important until you start building a life together and the older partner dies and leaves you alone. Or it's never important until you want to enjoy certain things in life that he's incapable of enjoying because of his age."

"If two people love each other, nothing else matters."

"I wish it was that simple, Deseret. Oh, how I wish it was that simple."

"Well, mother, it might be that simple if two people who love each other were left alone, if other people didn't cause complications in their lives."

Honey knew how to handle her strong-willed daughter, knew better than to force an issue. She also had confidence that Deseret would, in the final analysis, make the right decision. So she asked, "When will your father and I have opportunity to meet this wonderful man of yours?"

It was a question, but also an invitation to which Deseret quickly responded, "Whenever is best for you." She figured Brian would resist meeting her parents, but thought herself quite capable of convincing him to do what she wanted.

"Why don't you ask him to have dinner with us this week? Any evening will be fine. And try to find out his favorite foods."

Deseret was pleased. Her mother was the consummate hostess, and Brian would be treated to a meal fit for a king. Honey's abilities in the kitchen were suspect, but the family's Mexican cook Dolores was capable of preparing outstanding cuisine. It would be, she thought, a memorable evening.

"Let me know as soon as possible as to when he's coming," Honey said.

"I will. I'll probably talk to him tomorrow, Monday at the latest."

Honey jokingly said, "You might tell him to wear a bulletproof vest. Your father might not take kindly to an older man being interested in his daughter."

The statement caused Deseret to think about Brian's earlier call. With what's going on, she thought, he probably should be wearing a bulletproof vest, but not because of daddy.

"Daddy may not have anything to worry about. I may be more interested in him than he is in me."

"Pooh," Honey replied. "A man would have to be a fool not to be interested in you, and from what you've said about Professor Stratford, he's no fool."

I hope not, Deseret thought.

11

I didn't sleep very soundly, which isn't unusual when in a strange bed. The older I get, the greater the preference for things that are familiar.

I also rarely eat breakfast, but at eight o'clock found myself in the Ramada Inn coffee shop staring at the yellow eyes of two eggs over medium. Why I ordered two eggs, I'm not sure. I don't like them, but I occasionally think eating them would be good for me.

Anyway, I choked down some of the eggs, polished off my bacon and wheat toast without difficulty. Once the food was out of the way, it made reading the paper and drinking coffee a lot easier.

I'm always amazed at how little actual news there is in a newspaper, but I did find a couple of articles of interest on the front page. After checking out the business section, I stacked it along with all the other unwanted sections of entertainment and so on. The sports section was a little more interesting, but contained about eighty percent more verbiage than necessary; lots of garbage that would interest very few persons in Dallas.

As usual, in trying to have something for everyone, the

paper had missed the boat in providing coverage for the majority of its readers.

Though I had planned to get an early start cleaning up my apartment, the very thought of it depressed me. So I went back to the room and called Dave.

As soon as he identified my voice, he said, "Did you know Frank Becker and his wife were killed in an automobile accident last night?"

His informative question surprised me and started the wheels of suspicion turning in my mind. "No, I didn't. There was nothing about it in today's paper."

"I heard it on the radio a few minutes ago. They just recovered the car."

"Recovered the car from where?"

"From Lake Ray Hubbard."

Dave was making reference to a twenty-three thousand surface-acre reservoir just east of Dallas. Interstate Highway Thirty crosses it.

"No pun intended, but with what's happened that sounds a bit fishy."

"The minute I heard, I knew what your reaction would be," Dave said.

"Can you blame me?"

"Not really. The thought of foul play crossed my mind, too."

"Who recovered the car?"

"The Rockwall Fire Department."

Rockwall is a small city on the east side of the lake, about twenty-five miles from downtown Dallas.

"Were there any witnesses?"

"I don't know. If there were, they weren't mentioned on

the newscast."

"I think I'll go out to Rockwall to see what I can find out."

"I figured you'd be cleaning your apartment."

"It can wait. Besides, I have to buy a new mattress, pillows and all that kind of stuff. The stores don't open until ten."

"You know you're welcome to stay over here."

"Thanks, but you know I can't do that."

"Come by the house and I'll go with you."

"You'd better stay there and take care of Betty."

"She wants me out of her hair."

"Seriously, Dave, with what's happened, don't you think you should hang around the house?"

"You're probably right."

I soon had the old Ramcharger humming toward Rockwall. It's not the most beautiful vehicle in the world, slurps gasoline like desert sand swallows water, but it's as tough a vehicle as a man could want.

The day I took Deseret to lunch, I think she was a little embarrassed about riding in it. But hell, it's me.

At the Rockwall Fire Department Station, I talked to Tom Brown, one of the firemen responsible for pulling the Beckers' car from the water.

"Did anyone actually see the accident?" I asked.

"Not that we know of," he replied. "Early this morning a trucker saw the rear end of the car sticking out of the water and called it in. It must have happened real late last night or real early this morning."

"What time did the trucker call it in?"

"About daylight. Just a little of the rear end was

sticking out of the water, so it's not likely anyone could have seen it in the dark."

"Did you notice anything unusual at the scene?"

"No, but I really wasn't looking for anything unusual, either. It's not the first time someone's lost control of a car and ended up in the lake."

"Could you describe to me where you found the car?"

"I'll just run you out there. It won't take long."

Brown insisted on making the trip in his Chevrolet pickup, which is tricked out with just about every accessory imaginable. He's a square-jawed, sturdy-built man, with not an ounce of fat on what I judge to be about a six-foot frame.

It took no more than five minutes to find where the Beckers' car had careened off the road, over a good stretch of rock riprap, and into the water. There were no skid marks.

"You'd think he would at least have hit the brakes," I said.

Brown shrugged his shoulders. "You never know what a guy will do when he loses control of a car."

I had to agree. "I'd like to see the vehicle."

"No problem," my host said. He drove me to where a wrecker had towed the car.

The Becker car was a new Oldsmobile Ninety-Eight, which now looked as though it had crashed through a barrier and across several yards of riprap. However, the interior of the car was intact, indicating that if it had been a waterless crash, and if the Beckers had been wearing their seatbelts, they would still be alive.

"It doesn't look as though the crash killed them," I

said.

Brown grunted. "They drowned."

"Were they wearing seatbelts?"

"They were strapped in big as you please. Looked as though neither one of them even moved."

"Tell me, Tom, if you crashed into the water like they did, wouldn't you make an effort to get out of the car?"

"You bet, if I wasn't knocked unconscious."

"If you were securely held in by a seatbelt, why would you be unconscious? The windshield on this car isn't even damaged. If the seatbelts held properly, then neither victim would have hit their head on the dash or windshield. Yet from what you say, neither of them even tried to unbuckle their seatbelt and escape."

Brown pondered my words, then said, "Now that you mention it, that is a little strange. Maybe the strain of the seatbelts against their bodies when the car hit the water knocked the breath out of both of them."

"Not likely. Even if the breath is knocked from you, you still fight for your life."

"Okay," Brown said with a shrug of the shoulders, "maybe they were drunk, doped up, I don't know."

I laughed. "If I were drunk, I think I could still unbuckle my seatbelt. Since I've never had any dope, I don't know about that."

"Not even a joint?"

"Not even a joint."

"And I'll bet you're a Vietnam vet, too."

"That's right."

He shook his head in wonder. "That's amazing."

I walked to the rear of the car, pointed to the bumper

and said, "Look at that. It looks like something hit this car from behind."

"It sure as hell does," he agreed. "These wrecker guys, they could tear up a steel ball. They might be responsible for that bumper being pushed in."

"It looks as though it was done with another bumper," I said.

"Sure looks like it," Brown agreed.

"Did the Rockwall County Sheriff's Department or the Rockwall Police investigate the accident?"

Brown laughed. "Both were at the scene, along with the Department of Public Safety, the Dallas Police and the Garland Police." Garland is a town on the west side of the reservoir.

"It sounds like you had more than enough help."

"Yeah, we had cops running over each other. Most of them like to come out and watch us get our asses wet."

"Where were the bodies taken?"

"I imagine the Dallas County medical examiner has them."

I figured autopsies would be performed. Insurance companies tend to insist on it, especially when there are no witnesses to an accident. People have been known to load up on barbiturates, then try to make suicide look like an accident so as not to deprive their loved ones of insurance money. It works at times, usually in places where there's not a real coroner. But in or around Dallas County, which has one of the best forensic labs in the country, the bodies of dead folk can often be read like a book.

On the way to my apartment, I stopped at a pay phone

and called Deseret. She already knew about Franklin and Mrs. Becker.

"Daddy heard it on the radio and told me," she said. "It's awful. Do you think it was murder?"

"Maybe I'm just overreacting to what has happened, but yes, I think it was murder."

"Things are really getting scary," she said. Then she told me about the car that followed her home.

"You stay put," I commanded. "I don't want you zipping around town until I can get a few things organized."

"What are you going to do now?" she asked.

"I'm going to try to rake out my apartment and put it back together."

After Deseret got off the line, I called Dave and gave him a report on my findings at the lake.

"My suggestion is that you stay close to home, don't expose yourself to any unnecessary danger," I said. "With what happened last night, I don't want anyone I care about around me."

"That's good advice," Dave agreed.

I was maybe thirty minutes into cleaning up my trashed out apartment when the doorbell rang. Opening the door, I found Dave, Betty, and Deseret standing there.

"We're here to help," Dave said.

Some people just won't accept good advice.

I reluctantly agreed to have dinner with Deseret and her parents on Wednesday night. Perhaps because they realized I would be a bit uncomfortable, Dave and Betty were also invited.

The home of Alan and Honey Antares is most

impressive. It is a Southern colonial-style two-story with a half-dozen bedrooms and an equal number of full bathrooms. All the rooms are large.

In some rooms expensive oriental rugs partially cover highly polished hardwood floors, whereas posh carpeting fully covers the floors of other rooms. Eye-catching in the living room is a large and beautiful marble fireplace, which is accented perfectly by the room's furnishings.

However, it is impossible to describe the house and its contents with words. It's sufficient to say that the house and all that is in it is exquisite, tasteful, and speaks of wealth. It is truly a reflection of its owners.

"Deseret tells me that both of you teach journalism," Alan Antares said.

Dave and I were on the patio with Deseret's father, having a before dinner drink.

"I'm afraid we're guilty as charged," Dave replied jokingly. "Journalism was the only thing I could pass in college."

The response caused Antares to smile. He is a tall, lean and handsome man with graying hair. He has a Roman nose, and the honest lines and wrinkles expected of a man who is fifty-nine. He looks the perfect match for Deseret's mother.

"I don't know that much about journalism," he said, "but like a lot of business people I tend to think the press is too liberal."

My response was, "I agree with you about the press being too liberal. Of course, I'm a conservative. Dave here, he's a liberal."

Dave gave me a mock dirty look. "I'm pretty

conservative myself, Mr. Antares, it's just that Brian's politics are to the right of those practiced by Atilla the Hun."

Antares laughed, then asked that we not address him as Mister. "Call me Alan," he said.

We both complimented him on his home, to which he replied, "Honey and I had the house built quite a few years ago, back when prices in Highland Park weren't so inflated. Of course, at the time we anticipated having more than one child.

"The place is too big for us, but we're used to it now and I can't see much point in moving to something smaller."

Dave and I agreed with him that it would serve no good purpose to move.

"Deseret told me your apartment was vandalized."

"Yeah, someone did a pretty good job on it."

"She said she invited you to stay with us until you got it back in shape, but you refused."

"I'm sure you can understand that I would feel a bit uncomfortable staying in the home of persons I don't know."

"Well, you know us now," he said. "We have more than enough room and you wouldn't be any bother."

"That's very kind, but my place is in pretty good shape now. Hopefully, it won't be vandalized again."

"With all the meanness going on nowadays, you never can tell. Anyway, the invitation stands. Any friend of Deseret's is always welcome in our home."

It would be very difficult to dislike Mr. or Mrs. Antares. They reflect a grace, charm and caring that in today's world is in short supply. However, I'm not deceived into thinking they would treat everyone in the same manner they treat me. Because of my relationship with Deseret, they have given me special status.

"Would you like another drink?" Alan asked.

Both Dave and I gave different answers. While Alan mixed the drinks at a portable bar on the patio, he said, "Terrible thing about your dean, and about the journalism chairman and his wife."

The deaths of Franklin and Mrs. Becker had also been ruled suicides. Autopsies had revealed barbiturates in the system of both bodies, but the most telling evidence was a suicide note Becker had left in his office typewriter. The note had been typed and was unsigned, but the police were satisfied. I think most police satisfaction lies in being able to write CLOSED on a case file. There is, however, one detective, a Sergeant Mark Lightfoot, who shares my suspicions regarding the deaths of the Beckers. And I think he is even beginning to have some doubts about the death of Reginald Masters being a suicide.

In response to Alan's statement, though, I merely said, "The university has had more than its share of tragedy this fall."

Of course, he didn't let me get off so easily. "Deseret tells me you think all three deaths could have been murder."

Damn it, she wasn't supposed to say anything. "Oh, I tend to have a very suspicious nature."

"I'll testify to that," Dave said.

Alan persisted. "You must have some reasons for thinking these people were murdered."

"I don't have anything concrete. It's just that I don't

think Reginald Masters or Franklin Becker were the types to commit suicide."

Alan's brow furrowed. "Why is it that I think you know a lot more than you're telling?"

I was rescued when the women emerged from the house and joined us on the patio. Over the years, I've observed that when a group of women join a group of men in casual conversation, the female gender usually dominates. This time, I was grateful.

After a period of lighthearted conversation with drinks, Honey led us to the dining room and a large, beautiful table complimented by fine china and silver. The room was bathed in soft candlelight.

Alan nudged me, smiled and whispered, "Amazing isn't it. Women want the finest in light fixtures and lamps, but always seem to prefer candlelight."

I responded with a soft chuckle. "I don't claim to understand women, but I can't argue with the ambiance of this setting."

The meal was exceptional; fine beef that tasted like beef, not covered in some sort of sauce to destroy its flavor. The vegetables were steamed and also sauce-free, just the way I like them. And though not a connoisseur of fine wine, even I could understand the specialness of that which was served with the meal.

After dessert, coffee and more conversation, Dave and Betty left. Alan and Honey also excused themselves and sought refuge in another part of the house, leaving Deseret and me alone for the first time during the entire evening.

She kissed me lightly on the lips, filled our wine glasses

and led me out on the patio.

"Well, what do you think?" she asked.

"Dinner was great."

She sighed with resignation. "You know what I mean. What do you think of mom and dad?"

I laughed. "I think they're very nice. And they couldn't have treated me any better."

She smiled. "See, they're not ogres."

"I didn't think they would be, not and have a beautiful daughter like you. Beautiful but very hardheaded."

"Now what do you mean by that?" she asked in a mock half pout.

"You know damn well what I mean. With all that's been going on, I'm not sure it was wise for me to come here."

"Oh, pooh! You can't withdraw from everyone because you think you being with them might put them in danger. When would it end? And what can you really do about it?"

"I don't know. I just know that three people have been murdered and their deaths are going down as suicides."

"Did you see the note Professor Becker allegedly left? See, just like you I'm qualifying all my statements."

I like her sense of humor. "Yeah, I saw it. It really didn't say anything, except that Becker and wife were tired of life, which makes absolutely no sense. The man was a real nincompoop, but he was on top of his profession. And he had plenty of money, more really than he should have had on his salary."

Deseret put her wine glass on a table, put her arms around my waist and pulled me close, smiled and said,

"Have you been breaking into people's houses without me?"

I chuckled. "Well, I felt duty-bound to check out ol' Frank."

"Did you find anything?"

After giving her a gentle kiss, I said, "You ask too many questions."

"I wouldn't have to ask if you weren't so secretive."

"It's for your own good."

"You should let me be the judge of what's good for me."

"Not in this situation," I said. "But it's not something I'm going to argue about. Have you noticed anyone following you the last two or three days?"

"No, and I've been watching, too. Since Saturday night, there hasn't been anything unusual. What about you? Anything unusual since your apartment was trashed?"

"Nothing. Maybe they've decided I don't have what they're looking for."

"But you do, don't you?"

I still hadn't told Deseret, or anyone else, about the book I'd taken from Reg's house.

"I don't know what they're looking for," I lied.

"I know what you're doing," she said. "You think that by not telling me you're protecting me."

"There's nothing to tell."

"Well, what are you going to do about the murders?"

"What can I do? If the police are satisfied to rule the deaths suicide, then there's nothing I can do."

She smiled. "For some reason, I don't believe that."

I chuckled. "It doesn't matter what you believe, there's nothing I can do."

We chatted for awhile, then I left.

Though it was getting late, for some reason I was reluctant to go home. Maybe it's because my mind was running full throttle, forcing me mentally to deal with so much that had happened in so short a time. Foremost in my mind was Deseret, how I was going to handle our rapidly developing relationship.

I parked the Ramcharger in front of a donut shop, went in and ordered a cup of coffee. I certainly wasn't hungry, but the smell of freshly baked donuts was too much to resist. I ordered a couple.

While Alan and Honey Antares had been quite gracious, I knew they couldn't be all that pleased about their daughter being interested in a man of my ilk and age. Dinner at their home had made me realize I could never provide Deseret with the kind of life to which she was accustomed. Any kind of serious and continuing relationship was, to my way of thinking, hopeless. Though such an evaluation saddened me, experience has taught me it is best to face reality head-on and immediately.

Had I not been so engrossed in thought, I might have been more aware of the two men who entered the donut shop. My awareness level jumped into the danger zone when they chose to occupy counter stools right next to and on either side of me. Until their arrival, the shop was empty except for the baker and me. And he had just refilled my cup and gone to the back to check on some donuts.

I really didn't turn and look at either of the men, just out of the corner of my eye saw one reaching inside his coat for what I was sure was a gun. Simultaneously, I tossed hot coffee in the face of one and caught the other flush in the neck with an elbow. Both went backwards off the stools.

The victim of the blow grabbed his neck with both hands and fought to get air into his lungs. The other wiped coffee from his eyes with one hand and groped for the gun in a shoulder holster with the other. I gave him a groin kick that would have made an NFL punter proud. He doubled up in pain and started retching.

By this time the other man had recovered enough to reach for his gun. I put a shoulder in his chest that knocked him backward and through the shop's plate glass window. He screamed and I saw blood, but I didn't have time to check it out. My attention was back on the other man, who I then kicked in the face. He went sprawling against a wall and I went after him, pounding his face with my fists. When he was immobilized, I removed his gun from the shoulder holster and took refuge behind the counter.

With the pistol at the ready position, I moved to one end of the counter and cautiously looked through the broken window in an effort to find the other man. He was lying outside the window, groaning. He was a bloody mess.

After retrieving his gun, too, I told the baker to call the police and an ambulance. He was excited, shaken. "I've never seen anything like this," he said. "That'll teach these clowns to try to rob me."

If the man wanted to think the two oriental gunmen were merely robbers, it was fine with me.

12

Detective Sergeant Mark Lightfoot stands six feet tall and, though forty, still looks capable of running over or through a defensive line. During his college years at Howard Payne, he was a running back who operated behind a very poor offensive line. So, he's a man used to a little adversity.

I had gotten to know Lightfoot while trying to get information from the police regarding the deaths of Reginald Masters, Franklin Becker, and his wife. Although we had known each other for only a brief period of time, we had dispensed with all formalities and caution in our discussions.

"Damn it, Brian, why in the hell did you wait until now to tell me someone broke into your apartment?"

The police had earlier taken my statement regarding the two orientals who had allegedly attempted to rob the donut shop. I'd run into Mark afterward, and he'd asked me to have a cup of coffee with him.

"It didn't seem very important at the time," I replied. "If you'll recall, some of your colleagues didn't like me suggesting that Reginald Masters might have been murdered. They would really have gotten uptight if I'd suggested there might be some connection with the ravaging of my apartment and the death of Masters."

"Of course, that's a lot of speculation," Lightfoot said.

"Maybe so, but you have to admit it's quite a coincidence that the break-in was sandwiched in between the Masters and Becker murders."

"Damn it, Brian, will you get off that murder stuff? We don't know that Masters or the Beckers were murdered."

"*You* don't know. I do."

Lightfoot gave an exasperated shake of the head. "And you think these guys came into the donut shop tonight to waste you, not to rob the place."

"I don't think they wanted to waste me, at least not in public. I think they planned to take me somewhere and talk to me. If they had gotten the information they wanted, then they would have killed me."

"Well, the one who's still able to talk said they just came in the place for coffee and donuts and you attacked them," the detective said.

"What did you expect him to say? He's sure not going to admit to attempted murder."

"I'm not sure we'll be able to hold them at all, since they didn't actually pull their guns and demand money from the guy running the place."

"That doesn't surprise me. Did they have permits for the guns?"

"No, and there were no serial numbers on the guns, either. But you know how screwy the law is. You might turn out to be the heavy in this deal."

"The baker sure the hell thought they were there to rob

him."

"That's true, but when it comes right down to it, you didn't even give them a chance to try."

"This sounds a lot like Vietnam to me," I said. "We draw a line that we're not supposed to cross, but it's okay if the enemy wants to come across and take some shots at us."

"Brian, I don't like it any better than you do, but we really don't have much here. What we've got are two Vietnamese that you damn near killed. If they wanted, they could file charges against you. I'll be surprised if they don't get a smart lawyer and sue you."

"I'll make you a bet on that, Mark. My guess is that when you cut those guys loose, we'll never be able to find them again."

Lightfoot somberly said, "Look, you already know I have some suspicions about the deaths of Masters and the Beckers, but I don't have that much to work on. And, of course, the department has closed the book on all three deaths. I could get my tail in a crack for even thinking about reopening an investigation."

"The investigations of the deaths of Masters and the Beckers were really lightweight operations," I complained.

"I won't argue that, but I get the feeling you think there's some sort of major conspiracy. If you'd give me something to work with, maybe I could help you."

"Hell, I don't have anything."

"If you don't have anything, Brian, why do you think these two guys were after you? If you don't have anything, why do you think the break-in of your apartment has something to do with the deaths of Masters and the Beckers?"

"I can't help it if these people think I've got something."

"Who are *these people?*" the detective asked.

"How would I know?"

"I think you have a pretty good idea — you're just not saying."

"I'll make a deal with you, Mark. When I'm sure, you'll be the first to know."

Lightfoot grunted, as though he didn't particularly believe me. "You made some friends down here tonight."

"How's that?"

"Cops aren't allowed to say it, but we all appreciate it when a guy works a hood over."

"Hood? I thought there was a possibility I'd be arrested for what I did to a couple of upstanding citizens."

"You may be arrested," Lightfoot said, "but we know these guys aren't legit. We don't buy their story about going in the place for coffee and donuts. Your average citizen doesn't carry an unregistered firearm with no serial number. But if either of those guys wants to force the issue, a lawyer can probably nail you for violating their rights."

"If they come at me again, they won't be able to talk to a lawyer."

Lightfoot grinned. "I didn't hear that, but I doubt that they would try you again at close range. Those guys are so battered they look like they've been through a sausage grinder."

When I arrived at my apartment, I found it was once again in shambles. I figured the guys I'd worked over had made the mess, but the fact I'd already put both of them in the hospital wasn't satisfying. I wanted someone to hit at that moment.

Immediately after the incident at the donut shop, I had called Deseret. I was concerned for her safety and that of her parents. I didn't tell her about the two men, only that I suspected I had been followed and that she and her parents should exercise extreme caution.

She was suspicious. "Is there anything wrong?" she had asked.

"No, everything's fine. Just be careful."

Lying to her was becoming increasingly difficult. She was too atuned to my moods.

I had been in the apartment only a few minutes when the phone rang. It surprised me because it was one-thirty in the morning.

"I've been calling you for hours," Deseret said when I answered. "Where have you been?"

There was no reason to lie. "I've been down at the police station."

"What happened?"

"My apartment's been trashed again."

"I can't believe it," she said, obviously thinking the break-in was the reason for my trip to the police station.

"Believe it. If anything, it's worse than before."

"Brian, you just can't stay there any longer. I want you to come over here."

"We'll talk about that tomorrow, Dez."

"Daddy's already told you that you're welcome."

"Yes, and I appreciate it. But I'm not coming over there this late, okay?"

We argued for a few moments, then realizing she couldn't change my mind she said, "I'd feel safer if you were here with me."

"But you wouldn't be safer," I said.

Though I told Deseret I would go to a motel to get some sleep, I was too tired. I fell asleep on my new, ripped up mattress.

When I awoke Thursday morning from a short and fitful sleep, I was disgusted, angry, and determined to do something about Foster Cerney. I didn't know whether or not he was responsible for the deaths of Reginald Masters and the Beckers, but I was convinced he was behind the trashing of my apartment and the two thugs I had encountered in the donut shop.

There are those who accuse me of being too swift to anger, but in not going after Cerney I had been far too patient. It was time for a little weekend vacation to McCurtain County, Oklahoma.

After teaching my first morning class, I returned to my office and picked up my phone messages. There was one from Deseret's father. It was not a surprise. I had anticipated the call.

When I got Alan Antares on the line, he asked if I was free for lunch. I agreed to meet him at a restaurant near his office.

The invitation to lunch was no surprise, either. I also didn't think I'd be surprised by the reason for the invitation.

After doing some paperwork and teaching another class, I drove to the restaurant where we had agreed to meet. As usual, I was a bit early. Alan showed up right on time.

"Do you want a drink before lunch?" he asked.

"No, thanks. Ice tea is about the strongest thing I can handle at noon."

He chuckled. "I'm not much of a lunchtime drinker myself. But today I think I'll have a scotch and water."

Probably needs some reinforcement, I thought.

Our waiter brought him the drink while we were reading the menus.

"Have you decided?" Alan asked.

"Yeah, I'll have the chicken tenders."

"And I'll have the red snapper," he said.

After the waiter left there was a period of awkward silence before Alan said, "I'm glad you were free to meet me today."

"Well, it was nice of you to ask. I enjoyed meeting you and Mrs. Antares last night. The dinner was excellent."

"Honey really knows how to entertain," he said.

"She's a beautiful, charming woman. It's easy to see why Deseret is so beautiful."

"Deseret is beautiful, isn't she? And young."

"Yeah," I said. "She's beautiful and she's young. She's much too young for me, which is why I think you wanted to meet me for lunch."

Alan was surprised by my statement, but relieved, I sensed, that he had been spared any preliminary verbiage in getting to the topic he wanted to discuss. He chuckled, then said, "Deseret told me you were quite perceptive."

"I'm perceptive enough to know how I'd feel if my daughter was interested in a man who was nineteen years older, and especially one like me."

"I hope you understand that Honey and I have nothing against you personally," he said. "Our primary concern is the age difference, the fact that you're so much more mature than Deseret."

I gave him a bemused look and said, "I don't know about the maturity part, because there are times when I think I'm a long way from being mature. I do understand your concern about the difference in ages, and I assure you that you have nothing to worry about.

"Last night, after leaving your house, I did a lot of thinking about my relationship with Deseret. I realized that for me to even think in terms of a life with her was wrong. And it's not just the age thing, either. She's accustomed to a lifestyle that I could never provide. If I continue teaching, which I plan to do, I'm never going to be much better off financially than I am now. I don't think that's enough for Deseret."

Alan mulled my treatise, then said, "You obviously care a lot for Deseret, or you wouldn't be so concerned about what's best for her."

"Alan, I'll tell you something that I haven't even told Deseret. I'm in love with her, hopelessly, totally in love with her. It's because I love her that I'm willing to walk away."

"I really don't know what to say," he said.

"You don't have to say anything. There's something I think you should know, though."

"What?"

"Deseret and I . . . well, she's as pure today as the day I first met her. I've never taken advantage of her interest in me; never even tried."

"I already knew that," he said. "I not only trust my daughter completely, but from what she's told me about you, from the brief period in which I've known you, I'm convinced you are an honorable man."

The sincere way in which he said it took me off-guard. I gave an embarrassed half-laugh, then replied, "Well, I'm not all that honorable."

"I think you are. That's why in a lot of ways I'm sorry about this age thing. I think you'd take good care of Deseret."

"I'd damn sure try. But even if I was ten years younger, I still wouldn't have any money."

"Money isn't as important as you think," he said.

The waiter brought our food and we ate with limited conversation. There really wasn't much to say.

Back in my office at the university I tried to do a little typing, but my hands were too sore. It had been a long time since I had pounded anyone with my bare fists. And if I had my way, it would never happen again.

When I arrived at my office, there had been two phone messages from Deseret. I didn't bother to return her calls, so it was no surprise when I answered the phone and she was on the line.

"Didn't you get my messages?" she asked.

"Yeah, but I just got here. I haven't had time to return any calls."

"I just thought we might get together for a drink later this afternoon."

"I don't think so, Dez."

"What's wrong?"

"Nothing's wrong, except that I don't think it's a good

idea."

"If you're worried about someone bothering me if I'm seen with you, forget it. I'm being careful and I can take care of myself."

"I'm sure you can, but it's still not a good idea."

"What are you saying?"

"Dez, I'm saying that it's not a good idea for us to see each other. It wouldn't be a good idea if there hadn't been any trouble."

"This is a sudden change," she said, irritation in her voice.

"It's not all that sudden. From the very first I've felt that I was too old for you."

"Well, you're not. And I still don't know what brought all this on. I thought everything was all right last night. Did mother or dad say something to you?"

There was no reason to tell her about her father. "Last night was very enjoyable, but being at your home made me realize some things."

"What things?"

"Lots of things."

"That doesn't tell me anything."

"C'mon, Dez, let's not hassle. I told you seeing me isn't a good idea and that's all there is to it."

She whimpered, "Maybe for you. Don't you know I love you, Brian."

Her words hit me like a ton of bricks. "Don't talk crazy."

"It's not crazy. I do love you."

"You don't really even know me."

"I know you better than you think."

On my part there was silence, so she continued. "Okay, Brian, I'll leave you alone if you'll be honest with me. Is it a deal?"

"Sure," I said. "Why not?"

"I know you haven't told me, but if you can tell me you don't love me, I'll never bother you again."

It wasn't fair. The woman played dirty pool. "I'm not going to respond to something like that."

"You can't say you don't love me, can you?"

I didn't answer.

"The way I love you, Brian, I just know you love me. I'm sure of it."

"Damn it, Dez, I'm too old, too poor, too everything negative for you. And no matter what you say, I'm still going to walk away. I have to."

"No, you're not."

I couldn't help but laugh. "I sure as hell am."

She laughed, too. "You sure as hell aren't."

"You're unbelievable. Do you know that?"

"So I've heard," she said. "You may be a few years older than me, but —"

I interrupted, "A lot older than you."

"Well, you sure haven't learned much to be so advanced in years," she teased. "You still don't know what's best for you."

"And you do?"

"That's right."

"And what's best for me?"

"I am," she replied with laughter.

Until the phone call, I was relatively sure Deseret was *one* of the most hardheaded women I'd ever met. After trying to reason with her, I became convinced she *is* the most hardheaded woman I've ever known.

"It's okay if you don't want to have a drink with me this afternoon," she said, "but you're not going to get rid of me permanently. I'm not going to let you screw up something as good as you and me together."

Maybe I'm crazy, because Deseret had just told me all the positive things I wanted to hear from her. But in spite of my love for her, in spite of her professed love for me, I knew her father was right. I had made a commitment to him to no longer see Deseret on a personal basis.

I keep my commitments.

That evening, I once again made my apartment livable. I hadn't told anyone other than the police and Deseret about the second break-in. If at all possible, I wanted to keep the people I cared about, especially Deseret, out of the line of fire. I knew I was running the rim of a boiling cauldron, and also knew that in the not too distant future there was every possibility that all hell was going to break loose.

In fact, I planned to make sure it did.

The two orientals I had engaged in combat, I was sure, belonged to Cerney. He had used Vietnamese hoodlums to do his dirty work in 'Nam, so he was continuing to do so in the United States. Old habits are hard to break.

I wanted Cerney, wanted him bad. I realized getting him wouldn't be easy. In the past I'd had the resources of the Agency. Now I was alone.

13

On Friday night, all hell broke loose.

The entire day hadn't been one to file in my scrapbook of happy memories. I was depressed because of the decision to sever my relationship with Deseret. Lightfoot had called to tell me the Vietnamese thugs had been released on bail. They hadn't been charged with attempted robbery anyway, only with possession of illegal firearms.

I had eaten dinner, then settled in to watch a couple of inane dramas on the tube. A slow, cool October rain, the first real hint of winter, had moved into the area. It added the finishing touch to my already sour mood.

When the phone rang, I really figured the caller to be Deseret. For that reason, I considered not answering it. When I did, the caller's voice took me by surprise. It was the woman who had posed as Reginald Masters's sister.

"Mr. Stratford, I think you have something that belonged to my brother," she said. She was obviously unaware that I had uncovered her charade. I decided to go along.

"Sorry, Mrs. Wood, but I don't know what you're

talking about."

"He had a black book of names and addresses that was missing from his desk."

"Why do you think I'd know anything about it?"

"I have a very strong suspicion, Mr. Stratford, that you went through his things before I did."

"I can't imagine why you'd think that, Mrs. Wood. There was no reason for me to go through your brother's possessions. And I certainly didn't have a key to the house."

She sighed. "You're not going to make this easy, are you?"

"I don't know what I'm supposed to make easy."

"We know you have the book," she said.

"Who's we? You and Foster Cerney?"

There was silence, then. "Well, I wish there could have been an easier way, but you leave us no choice. Either give us the book, or we'll send your little sweetie to you in a body bag. You understand that kind of talk, don't you Mr. Stratford?"

The threat was easy enough to interpret, and I knew it was real. "Does this mean you're no longer playing the role of the grieving sister?"

Her laugh was sinister. "So, you know?"

"Yeah, I know. What I don't know is the location of this black book you're talking about."

"My suggestion is that you find its location."

I laughed. "And if I don't?"

In an icy voice, she said, "Mr. Stratford, before you find all this too amusing, do you know where I'm calling you from?"

"Well, Ms. Whoever You Are, I'm not a mind reader. If I were, maybe I could find this black book you're so interested in."

"I'm calling from the Antareses' home," she said.

Her words chilled me. There was no reason to doubt her. I knew the kind of people with whom I was dealing. They had already deep-sixed three persons I knew. Three more wouldn't make any difference to them.

In such situations, the hero always says something like, "If you dare hurt her, I'll kill you." However, not feeling like much of a hero, and not wanting to antagonize the woman, I said, "Look, let's try to work this thing out. Maybe you could take me, let the Antares family go."

"I was told you'd probably want to make a swap," she said. "But it's no deal. The only swap I'll make, Mr. Stratford, is the book for their lives."

Her demand left me with absolutely no choice. Even if the information in the book was the only way I could nail Cerney, it was too high a price to pay. The phony Julia Woods knew that. In fact, I was certain she knew much more about me than I knew about her.

I was more than willing to trade her the book for the lives of her captives, the only problem being that it was Friday night and the book was in a bank safety deposit box. The bank would be open the following morning, but what about Deseret and her parents in the meantime? I couldn't really trust Cerney's people to leave them unharmed even if I delivered the book. The man's history was one of leaving dead bodies, not live witnesses.

"How do we work the exchange?" I asked.

"I don't suppose you'd want to just come here and

bring the book?"

"You suppose right," I said. "When I deal with you, lady, it's going to be where I at least have a chance to see the light of one more day."

She laughed. "I would have been disappointed if you had just brought the book over. It would have destroyed my illusion, all I've heard about you."

"You obviously know the book's not in my apartment or office."

"You're right, I do know that."

"It's in a safety deposit box, and I can't get to it until nine o'clock in the morning."

There was a long silence, then she said, "I belive you, simply because having it in a safety deposit box makes good sense. We already know you didn't tell the police about it."

"That's right. I'm the only one who knows about it. I didn't even have sense enough to give my lawyer a letter to deliver to the authorities in the event of my death."

She laughed again, then in a somber tone said, "Then I don't have to tell you how stupid it would be to try to rescue your friends? And I'm sure you also know how futile it would be to involve the police or any of your old Agency cohorts?"

"I'm sure you have the Antares home well secured," I replied.

"And the family is cooperating beautifully," she said. "Mr. Antares has made sure his security service won't bother us. The only real danger to the family is you, Mr. Stratford. Hopefully, you won't do anything foolish."

"What can I do?"

"I've been told that you're somewhat reckless," she said.

"Maybe with my life, but not with the lives of others."

"I'm glad to hear that. Now, what about the exchange."

"You're asking for a suggestion from me?"

"Surprised?"

"Yeah, a little."

"Well?"

"I pick up the book at the bank a little after nine. Then I drive over to the east parking lot of Valley View Mall. I park near Dillard's Department Store and you and your people park about a hundred yards directly south, which I guess would be near Sears.

"You walk toward Dillard's and I'll intercept you. I give you the book, then your people start the Antares family walking toward Dillard's. You start walking back toward your people."

"Ingenious," she said, "and I don't guess the stores in the mall will be open at that time?"

"They open at ten, so there won't be many cars in the parking lot."

"What's to keep me from just taking the book and walking away, not allowing your friends to go free?"

"Since you know so much about me, you probably know something of my ability with a pistol. You probably also know that I wouldn't experience a second's hesitation in blowing your brains out."

I knew she was using an old terrorist ploy. She had allowed me to dictate a plan, but she was not going to accept it.

"Here's what we're going to do," she said. "At eight

forty-five in the morning, I'll call you and give you a phone number. When you've picked up the book, you'll call the number and I'll tell you when, where, and how the exchange will be made. And be assured, Mr. Stratford, that you will be watched."

"I wouldn't have it any other way," I said.

There was, in all probability, someone watching the apartment at that very moment. That person, or persons, would have to be taken out, because there was no way I was going to leave Deseret and her parents in the clutches of the phony Julia Wood and a cadre of what I was sure were Vietnamese thugs.

Fortunately, my apartment was on the second floor of the two-story complex. Because of my previous nonacademic career, before leasing it I had checked for escape routes. That's when I discovered the dandy attic crawl space that enabled me to traverse the entire building and exit at the other end.

Once on the ground, it was easy enough to check out all the cars offering a view of my apartment. Sure enough, one of those cars held a man whose eyes were glued to the door of my abode.

The rain, which I had partially blamed earlier for my black mood, now befriended me. It aided my stealthful approach on the enemy. The rain and colder weather had also fogged up the car's outside mirrors, so it was easy enough to move in from behind and ultimately be crouching alongside the door on the driver's side.

It would have been easy to raise up and put a bullet in the man's head, but that's not my way. I guess I still suffer from that old western syndrome where, being the good guy, I have to let the bad guy draw first.

Which is one of my more stupid traits.

On this occasion, I had brought another weapon; a real odds evener. So when I stood to my feet, I hit his window full force with a thirty-six-inch, thirty-six-ounce Ted Williams model Louisville Slugger. I think the initial blow of the bat attack gave the guy a heart attack, but just to be sure I also pool cued him flush in the face with the big end.

Blood from his nose spurted everywhere. Needless to say, he was out like a light.

I've had the bat since high school, a relic of when I thought the longer and heavier the bat, the further and harder I could hit a baseball. I was grown before I realized its weight was the reason why I was so often a strikeout victim.

The man with the bloody face was oriental, Vietnamese I guessed. Anyway, I dragged him into the apartment and tied him up.

In motion picture and television dramas, heroes and villains who are tied up are always freeing themselves. When I tie someone up, the only way he can free an arm or leg is to chew it off.

I would need very little for my attack on the group holding Deseret and her parents hostage. A few simple tools of the trade would suffice. Most important was the ability to strike quickly, because my attempt to rescue the captives probably wouldn't surprise the captors; at least, not if the woman knew as much about me as she seemingly knew. Cerney would have alerted her that such rescue operations were an integral part of my former training.

My action would place Deseret and her parents in severe danger, possibly even cause their deaths. However, I was convinced that delivery of the book the next day would be a death warrant for all of us anyway.

I parked the Ramcharger several blocks from the Antares home and proceeded on foot. Fortunately, the house is on a very large lot with a large number of trees. There is, of course, also considerable shrubbery and ground cover. A creek runs across the back end of the lot, which is heavily wooded. I surmised the enemy would think that would be the direction from which I would come.

My guess was that the captive force would consist of no more than four men and the woman. The only positive thing in my favor was the fact that she wanted me alive, until the book was delivered. The book was also providing temporary safety for the Antares family, because the woman knew I wouldn't deliver if they were harmed.

Of course, I couldn't count on the woman explaining the need to keep me alive to her Vietnamese helpers.

I approached the house from the front, slithering across the grass and ground cover, utilizing trees and shrubs for cover. While I was sure the enemy would figure me to come in from the rear, I wasn't stupid enough to think they would leave the grounds in front of the house unprotected. Therefore, it came as no surprise when I touched it.

Even in the light of day, touching a trip-wire for explosives gives me a chill. At night, the chill is greater.

After traversing the wire, I decided the woman might not be as concerned about my safety as I'd previously concluded. It also sensitized me to greater awareness of other booby traps.

I found a couple more little surprises along the way, but easily disengaged them. These Vietnamese were either lazy, or didn't possess the expertise of the Viet Cong with whom I had become so familiar. Of course, Cerney's troops were probably South Vietnamese; real sissies by Viet Cong standards.

Still, the ease with which I was able to approach the house bothered me. The woman knew something of my disabilities. Maybe they planted their little traps knowing I'd find them. Maybe they now had me trapped.

I was now alongside the house and in some shrubbery. Since most of the light was coming from the kitchen area, I figured that's where Deseret and her parents were being held. The captors were probably eating, drinking and, in typical terrorist fashion, taunting their captives.

Moving cautiously, I worked my way to where I could see through one of the large kitchen windows. Deseret, Alan and Honey were sitting at a table. One of the captors was sitting at the end of the table, facing them. He had a bottle of beer in one hand, an automatic weapon lying in his lap.

Dolores, the Mexican cook and maid, was standing at the stove, obviously cooking something. Another of the captors was directly across the room from the stove, sitting in a chair tilted back against the wall. He also had an automatic weapon across his lap. Dolores's husband, who worked for the Antareses, too, was bound and sitting on the floor to the right of the captors.

There had to be others. But where? Where was the phony Julia Wood?

The good part of the kitchen scene was that Deseret, Honey, Dolores, and Alan weren't bound. The bad part was that I couldn't use my sawed-off shotgun. With so many innocents in such close proximity to the enemy, there was too great a danger of taking out one or more of the hostages.

Strangely enough, silly things always come to mind when I'm about to do something dangerous. In this situation, I thought about swinging in through the kitchen window on a rope; making like Tarzan. Of course, I didn't have a rope. There was nothing to tie it to anyway.

So, I positioned myself a few yards from the window, got a running start and crashed through it.

When I hit the table it went forward and into the guard who was sitting at its end. He went crashing backward across the room. The man sitting in the tilted chair seemed frozen momentarily, but then came to his feet and tried to turn his weapon in my direction. By then a nine millimeter slug from my automatic had caught him full in the chest. He toppled backward against the wall.

When I came crashing through the window, the hostages all hit the floor. They were still there, with exception of Deseret. I don't know where she got it, it all happened so quickly, but when the man hit with the table tried to put his gun on me, she hit him full in the face with a pot of hot coffee. He screamed and I clubbed him unconscious with the butt of my gun.

I looked at Deseret and she held up two fingers, telling me what I wanted to know. There were two more of the enemy in the house. I quickly doused the kitchen lights, putting the room in almost total darkness.

We were all on the floor now. I positioned myself where I could see through the door leading into the dining room and waited. They had no choice but to come after us. I could only hope they weren't armed with fragmentation grenades.

I had brought the shotgun through the window with me, so I knew I could cover the door. My only concern was that they might come from different directions.

The two appeared almost simultaneously, one in the dining room and one outside at the window, raking the kitchen with automatic weapons fire. The man in the dining room caught a full load from the shotgun, but before I could turn to fire at the window, the man there caught several rounds fired by an automatic weapon from inside the kitchen.

It was Deseret who pulled the trigger. She had used a gun belonging to one of her captors.

We all lay there in silence for a few minutes, then I whispered, "Is that all of them?"

"Yes," Deseret said.

"Anybody hurt?" I asked.

Everyone reported they were okay, Dolores while sobbing. When I turned on the light, it was obvious that Honey was quite shaken. Alan, on the other hand, seemed calm enough. And Deseret was flushed with the excitement of the moment. Manuel, Dolores's husband, just sat there staring, stunned.

"We got them," Deseret almost shrieked. "We got every damn one of them."

I'd seen young men act the same way in 'Nam, ecstatic after their first firefight. There is something about such a close encounter with death that makes a person feel more alive than at any other time in their life. However, I knew that when the glow of victory dimmed, Deseret was in for a bad time. She had killed a man, and the reality of what she had done would soon begin to haunt her. And it wouldn't matter that the man had been trying to kill us. Taking a human life, even of an enemy, hurts. It makes us realize our frailty, our inability to deal with other human beings in an intelligent way.

"Where's the woman?" I asked.

"She left right after talking to you," Alan said, his voice now indicating he was shaken by what had happened. "My god, I thought we were goners."

Deseret had come and put her head on my chest, her arms around me. I put an arm around her shoulders.

"I knew you'd come," she said.

I directed an apology to Alan. "I'm sorry about this. I didn't want your family involved in this mess."

He was holding Honey close. "It's not your fault, Brian. When you're dealing with animals, you never know what they'll do."

"You'd better call the police," I suggested. "Ask for Sergeant Mark Lightfoot. Tell him to be careful coming in. There are some booby traps in the yard."

Uniformed officers arrived first, then Lightfoot and a couple of other plain clothes detectives. After surveying the situation, seeing one injured and three dead orientals, he asked, "What in the hell are you trying to do, Stratford, start the Vietnam War again?"

"Maybe," I grunted. "But this time they drew the line, and nobody's going to keep me from crossing it. By the way, there's another one in my apartment who's in pretty bad shape."

14

In the aftermath of Friday night's violence, Detective Lightfoot interrogated me for more than one hour. I told him about Foster Cerney, about my suspicions that Cerney was responsible for taking the Antares family hostage and for breaking into my apartment. He responded as I knew he would, with the question, "Why?"

I wasn't ready to give up the book, so I played dumb. With a shrug of the shoulders I replied, "I have no idea."

Because they had heard the phony Julia Wood in her telephone conversation with me, Deseret and her parents knew about the book. But prior to being questioned by police, I had asked them not to reveal its existence.

"I don't know why you don't want us to tell, and at this point I don't even care," Alan said. "I'm sure you have a good reason, so we'll go along."

To tell the truth, I wasn't sure myself as to why I wanted to keep the book a secret. Maybe it was just the gnawing anger inside me, the determination to take Cerney down myself. Or maybe it was because I knew local police didn't have jurisdiction where Cerney was holed up. They would, of course, eventually turn the material over to federal authorities. Whatever, the wheels of justice would turn too slowly to suit me.

"Frankly, Brian, I think you know a lot more than you're telling," Lightfoot said. "Whoever broke into your apartment was looking for something. The Antareses were obviously being held to smoke you out. If you'll tell me what's going on, maybe I can help."

"I've told you everything I know," I lied. "It all has to do with the murders of Reginald Masters and the Beckers, but I don't know why Cerney's after me."

Lightfoot shook his head in resignation. "Damn it, Brian, you just have to play like you're the Lone Ranger, don't you?"

I laughed. "Cut me some slack, Mark. When I know something, you'll know something.

"In the meantime, we do have an all points out on the woman who orchestrated holding the Antareses as hostages. I wish you'd told me earlier that she posed as Reginald Masters's sister."

"That was a mistake on my part. I think, though, that she's probably back across the Red River by now." The river is a boundary between Texas and Oklahoma.

"The deal with the Antareses put her on the federal hit list," Lightfoot said. "They'll get her."

"Don't hold your breath. If I wanted to hide, I can't think of a better place than in the southeastern part of Oklahoma."

"And you think she's linked to Cerney, so you think she'll be where he is?"

"That's right."

"This Cerney, from what you've told me he's real

garbage. Still, you don't have one shred of evidence that he's linked to what happened to Masters and the Beckers, or to the Antareses."

"Mark, there are certain things you just know. By the way, are the police going to continue treating Masters's death, and the Beckers deaths as suicides?"

"From an official standpoint, probably. But at least one cop is going to be taking a harder look at both cases."

"I appreciate it."

"I take my job seriously," he said, "which is why I'm still concerned about you and the Antareses. For god's sake, be careful. And consider trusting me a little more. I can probably help you a lot more than you think."

"Thanks for your concern, Mark, but I think everything is under control now. I don't think the Antareses will be bothered again, and I don't think I will be, either."

Of course, I didn't believe what I told Lightfoot. I figured Cerney would be more determined than ever to get the book, and that he would come after me again.

I continued, "However, for a while I think it would be good if you gave the Antareses police protection."

"I plan to do just that," he said, "though I probably can't guarantee it for more than a week."

"That should be adequate." I planned to give them a little protection of my own.

"What about this Antares girl, is she someone you're interested in?" Lightfoot asked.

Possibly too suspiciously I replied, "Why do you ask?"

Lightfoot grinned. "No reason. She's a real looker, maybe the best looking woman I've ever seen. And she's damn sure interested in you."

"What makes you say that?"

"C'mon, Brian, it's obvious to anyone who's around the two of you. And if you think you're not interested in her, you're lying to yourself. When the two of you are in the same room, the sparks fly."

"Hell, Mark, I'm almost twice as old as she is."

"Where have you been?" he asked. "People don't pay that much attention to age difference nowadays."

"Some people don't," I said. "I've already played a small part in raising a couple of kids."

"If you think she's a kid, you're a lot stupider than I think you are. She's one tough young lady, and you could sure do a helluva lot worse."

"And she could do a helluva lot better."

"I can't argue with you on that score," he said. "Anyway, for what it's worth, I think you two make a good team."

"There are those who say I've never been much of a team player."

"Those who say that are probably right. I sure as hell don't get much cooperation from you. But if I were you, Deseret Antares is a young lady I'd be reluctant to let get away."

If Lightfoot only knew. I had been lamenting the decision to let her go from the time I told her father I would do so. I did think it best under the circumstances, but it hurt just the same. Maybe my decision not to pursue her on a romantic basis had to do with a lack of confidence and self-esteem on my part. Though lack of confidence was never a problem for me in most of life's decisions, the age thing and her beauty could subconsciously have created some self-doubt.

Deseret had, of course, told me she loved me. But anyone can say the words. God knows, I've said them, then later regretted having done so. Love is, after all, such a difficult thing to define. Her definition of it, the implications of the definition, might be far different than mine.

For her, I might be just a whim, a fantasy to be fulfilled and then rejected.

There's very little in life I fear. To be honest with myself, I'm forced to admit I fear rejection. Fighting rejection is a "no win" proposition. It devastates the psyche.

Then there's the money thing. Hell, the girl's parents are wealthy, she's used to the best, and me, I'm used to making do. There was a time I aspired to money and fame, but that time is past. I have, hopefully, finally found my place in education.

So, while Lightfoot gave me some advice I wanted very much to follow, I had reservations about, and reasons for not, making such a commitment. If Deseret wanted my friendship, it was for the asking. If she wanted romance, I would have to say no.

Brave words.

Therefore, when she called me on Saturday afternoon, I had made considerable mental preparation to deal with her contentions that togetherness was right for us. She immediately ambushed me with, "Last night daddy told me he had talked to you about us. He said he was wrong to have done so."

"Maybe not so wrong, Dez. He's just trying to do what's best for you."

"I'm old enough to know what's best for me," she said. "But I'm not going to beg you to see me, Brian. I would like to see you tonight, because I'm feeling a little funny about all that's happened."

I figured remorse for the man she had shot was beginning to set in. I figured I was probably the best person for her to talk to regarding the incident.

Admittedly, I just wanted to see her.

When I showed up at the Antares home at five-thirty, there was no visible evidence that it had the evening before been in a war zone. Both Alan and Honey greeted me warmly.

"Deseret will be down in just a few minutes," he said. "How about a drink?"

I agreed to a light beer, then suggested, "Why don't you and Honey go along with us? We're just going out for dinner."

Honey laughed. "Frankly, Brian, I think we'd both just like an evening of peace and quiet here at home. We're still trying to recuperate from last night."

Alan smiled, then in somber tone said, "I'm not sure we adequately thanked you for what you did last night."

"There's nothing to thank me for. If it wasn't for me, you wouldn't have been involved in the mess."

"Maybe," Alan said, "but that's really not the point. The point is that we were in trouble and you responded. And you responded in a way that few people would have, at the risk of your own life."

His gratitude embarrassed me. He noticed and

attempted to make me feel more at ease.

"Anyway, Honey and I think Deseret is safer with you than anywhere else she could be. We know you'll take care of her. And we both regret initiating the talk I had with you the other day."

I quickly replied, "You shouldn't. What you said made good sense. You can count on me to be Deseret's friend. And yours, too. The reason I'm here is that I think she may be troubled because of the guy she shot last night. Maybe I can help her through any guilt or remorse she's feeling."

Honey smiled. "I can't say how she's feeling about that, but I know she's excited about seeing you. And I don't think you can keep Deseret from being more than just your friend."

Alan nodded agreement. "Honey and I have talked it over, and if things work out between you and Deseret, we're sure not going to stand in the way."

Moments later, Deseret came down the stairs. As always, she was dressed to perfection, the clothes simple and tasteful; ornaments to highlight her beauty. The four of us chatted for awhile, Alan and Honey again declined an invitation to join us, then we left.

In the Ramcharger, I turned to her and said, "You look beautiful tonight."

"Thank you," she replied, then leaned toward me and kissed me lightly on the lips.

I soon had the vehicle moving northward along one of the city's busier streets, which still showed some evidence of the night's rain. The temperature was cool, probably in the high fifties.

After a time, city traffic, commercial buildings and the usual semi-completed road construction gave way to a more pastoral setting. The sun had already dropped beyond the horizon, but its rays painted clouds an apricot color on a canvas of blue sky. Cows could still be seen shuffling along, grazing, in pastures alongside the road.

We had been making small talk, and Deseret didn't change the mood when she asked, "Up until now I haven't bothered to ask, but where are you taking me?"

"Into the boonies. It's a surprise."

"It looks to me like we're already in the boonies," she said. "What's the matter, Brian, are you ashamed to be seen with me in a Dallas restaurant?"

I laughed. "Dez, I'd never be ashamed to be seen with you anywhere."

"C'mon, I want to know where we're going."

"Just relax and enjoy the scenery."

"It's getting too dark to see. And so far all I've seen are cows and massage parlors."

There are, possibly, a half dozen massage parlors on the highway we were traveling.

"Okay, so the scenery's not that great on this stretch of the road," I said with a chuckle. "But it gets better."

"Good. Someday you can bring me out here when it's not too dark to see the terrain." Then her tone turned more serious and she said, "How long have you known about us?"

"What do you mean?"

"I mean, how long have you known there was something special between us?"

Her question was one I didn't want to answer, but there

was no place to hide. In terms of my feelings for her, I had been doing too much hiding.

"You affected me the first time I ever saw you," I said.

"Are you sure?"

"Of course, I'm sure. It's not something I'm likely to forget."

"Then why do you keep trying to avoid me?"

I sighed. "There are a lot of reasons, Dez, but I doubt that you really want to understand them."

She surprised me with, "I probably don't. And you're right, Brian, in thinking that I'm used to having things my way. Most of the boys I've dated were ready to jump at my command. You're more of a challenge."

"And that may really be all I am."

She defensively responded, "I didn't mean it that way. Damn, I hate it when I don't say what I mean."

I laughed. "Hey, don't worry about it. Everyone's guilty of that." Then trying to turn the conversation, I asked, "Have you ever been to Frisco?"

With attempted good humor, she asked, "San Francisco? Is that where we're going? Are you driving me to San Francisco for dinner?"

Chuckling, I said, "I'm talking about this little town we're coming into. I'm talking about Frisco, Texas."

"I don't think I've ever had the pleasure. Is it famous or something?"

"Not that I know of. It's where we turn, though."

"Oh, are we going further into the country to check out more massage parlors? By the way, are all massage parlors in trailer houses?"

"How would I know? I'm not an authority on massage

parlors." If I haven't mentioned it, there are those who contend massage parlors are nothing more than houses of prostitution. I wouldn't know, since I've never needed a massage.

She chided, "I don't guess you would be, not with all the sweet young things at school chasing you."

Her statement was discomforting. "I wasn't aware I was being pursued. I certainly haven't been caught."

"Don't play dumb with me. You know a lot of the girls on campus like you."

"And I like a lot of the girls, as students. I don't date students, Dez. At least, I haven't."

"But you've had lots of women. Lots and lots of women."

The conversation was making me uneasy. "I was married until a couple of years ago." I didn't want to think about other women. I didn't want her thinking about me being with other women. I didn't want to think about her being with any other man.

"I know you were married," she said. "But there have been other women since, and probably during your marriage."

I shrugged my shoulders. "You seem to know a great deal about us."

"People talk, especially at the university."

"Well, I can't do much about the talk and I can't change the past. The most important thing is, what do you really know about me?"

"I don't guess I know much," she admitted. "You are quite a topic of conversation at school. The students and teachers all talk about you."

"I don't know what they can say. I keep my personal life very private."

She smiled. "Oh, it's mostly speculation. You're a very attractive man and you turn a lot of women on, whether by design or not, I don't know. The male students and teachers can't decide whether to admire or despise you."

"I don't give a damn either way."

"And neither do I," she said, leaning over and kissing me on the cheek.

I wanted to pull her close, to kiss her passionately, but the narrow, winding road in front of me prevented it. I had, of course, chosen the route and restaurant because no one could follow us without being discovered. I had been keeping as close an eye on the rear view mirror as on the road ahead. We hadn't been followed, but I knew better than to let my guard down with Cerney still out there.

When I parked the Ramcharger in front of the Red Carpet Restaurant at Little Elm, Texas, I said, "This place has the best fried catfish in the world."

"I don't like catfish," she replied.

Inside the restaurant, we ordered a bottle of wine and she said, "We should have some sort of toast since this is a special occasion."

"You make the toast."

"I'd like to toast your asking me out, but as usual I had to ask you."

I groaned. "C'mon, that's not entirely true."

"Oh, yes it is. Regardless, my toast is...to us."

We touched glasses, then drank. And I feasted on the promise in her eyes.

We ordered food, but there was too much magic in the moment to be hungry. We held hands, drank wine, spoke softly about our feelings. I must have said, "I love you," because I heard her say, "I love you, too."

It was all a bit crazy, and I knew it. Here we were in a busy, family-type restaurant in the middle of nowhere, and we were oblivious to all around us. The noise, the hustle and bustle of the place, was all lost on us. We were in our own world.

After dinner we drove to Lake Dallas, parked, talked and watched the moon, like a big orange balloon, paint rippling water in varying hues of soft color. It was such a different night than the previous one, clear and peaceful. It was easy to forget that the dangerous forces of Friday night still lurked in the shadows.

It was still relatively early when we arrived back in the city, but neither of us were ready to go home. We went to Cappucino's, a small bar, had a couple of drinks and listened to music. I took Deseret home about one-thirty.

Still not sleepy, on the way home I stopped at the donut shop where I had dispatched the two orientals. The same guy was on duty who had been there when the incident happened. When he saw me come through the door, he grinned and said, "I hope you're not planning on breaking any heads or windows tonight."

I sighed. "You're not the only one. Frankly, I just don't feel up to it."

"By the way, it was the owner, not me, who insisted that you pay for the window," he explained.

I had almost forgotten that I'd had to pay for the plate glass window through which one of the orientals exited, with my help. It took all my meager savings to pay for the damage.

"Yeah, amazing isn't it. Hero one minute, vandal the next."

"Well, I still think they were going to rob me," the man said. "If you hadn't taken them out, I might even be a dead man. It's too bad the boss wasn't here, or he might look at things a little differently."

"Don't worry about it," I said. "I've still got enough for a cup of coffee and a couple of donuts."

He laughed. "That's where you're wrong. When I'm here, you get free coffee and donuts."

"That's not necessary."

"I insist."

I had polished off the donuts, was working on a second cup of coffee and thinking about Deseret when the man and woman came in. Both were dressed in western attire, which made me think they'd probably been to one of the country and western clubs in the area. They sat down at the end of the L-shaped counter, making it impossible for me not to be looking at them, which, as it turns out, was the reason for the trouble.

She was a pretty enough woman, but definitely not in the same class as Deseret. He was probably younger than he looked, maybe even in his late twenties but with enough belly to indicate a love for beer and pizza.

"What are you looking at?" he growled.

"I assume you're talking to me?"

"I sure as hell don't see anyone else in here."

"Well, in answer to your question, I'm not looking at anything in particular."

"I think you're staring at my girl." She was embarrassed, tugging at his sleeve and trying to get him to calm down. He was, however, obviously drunk.

"You're wrong, but from where you're sitting I'm almost facing you. It's impossible not to look at you and your girl."

He wasn't interested in logic. He got up off his stool and came toward me.

"I think, maybe, you need a lesson, big eyes," he said.

I sure wasn't going to sit there and let him play drums on my head, so I greeted his bull-like approach with a kick to the groin and an elbow to the neck. He went toppling backward and crashed through the plate glass window.

15

Pre-dawn, and once again I found myself having coffee with Detective Lightfoot, who jokingly said, "If I were you, I'd stay out of donut shops."

"The guy's going to be all right, isn't he?"

"He's fine. A few cuts and bruises, that's all. He was drunk as a skunk, probably didn't feel a thing. Since you weren't going to press charges, he's been released from the hospital and has gone home."

"Hell, I feel bad about it, but —"

Lightfoot interrupted. "Of course, there's the problem of who's going to pay for the plate glass window. I imagine the donut shop owner is going to look to you again for that."

I groaned. "Great. The last window cost me every cent I had."

Lightfoot laughed. "Like I said, stay out of donut shops."

At home I grabbed a little sleep, only to be awakened by the ringing of the telephone. It was Dave.

"Rise and shine," he said cheerfully. "Betty and I want you to join us for brunch."

"Forget it. I'm wiped out." I gave him a brief rundown on what had happened at the donut shop.

"It looks to me like you need to stay out of donut shops," he said.

"Funny, but you're too late to be original. I've already heard it."

"Well, you need to get up and stir around. If you stay in bed you'll get a headache."

"Worse than the one I have now?"

"C'mon, Betty's not taking no for an answer. She said if you didn't get moving, she'd come and give you a shower herself."

"Tell her to come ahead. She's got a lot of gall, but not that much."

"We'll pick you up in thirty minutes."

"I'm not going."

"Bye," Dave said.

I laid there for a few minutes, then decided I'd better get ready. I didn't think Betty was strong enough to physically give me a shower, but I decided it was best not to take a chance.

Dave's knock at the door came about thirty minutes later and I was ready. Betty, obviously thinking she had put the fear of God into me, hadn't accompanied him to the door.

I was surprised to find Deseret sitting in the back seat of the McPhersons' car.

"We decided you needed a brunch date," Betty said.

"You're too good to me," I grumbled.

"Is that a complaint?" Deseret asked. "Are you being facetious?"

"Of course not. I'm glad to see you, Dez. It's these other two clowns I could do without."

Dave laughed. "If it wasn't for us, you'd be lying in bed sound asleep."

"Yeah, and it would be wonderful."

After brunch at the Lincoln Hotel, Dave drove to Turtle Creek, where we did a little picture-taking and walking. The fall air was crisp, but not cold. The leaves on the trees were making their seasonal changes. It was a beautiful day, made more so for me because of Deseret's company. And, of course, it was good to be with friends like Dave and Betty.

Betty spread a blanket, Dave opened a bottle of good wine, and we toasted the day and the future.

For me, wine is a dangerous drink. After two or three glasses I was ready to assume a position parallel to and completely on the blanket. But my friends wanted to talk, and they droned on about a lot of Mickey Mouse nonsense. Then the ever troublesome Betty suggested that all of us should go to San Antonio the following weekend.

Normally, I could have made a completely logical excuse for not going, but the wine... Anyway, I said, "I have to go to Oklahoma next weekend."

They all stared at me in what looked like disbelief, but I rallied to continue, "I'm going fishing with a friend up there. I promised him some time ago."

In unison they said, "Liar."

Dave shook his head slowly and said, "So you're going after Cerney, huh?"

"I said I was going fishing."

"We know what you said," Deseret chimed in. "But please forgive us if we don't believe you."

It was Betty's turn. "Brian, you have no idea what you'll run into up there if half of what you told Dave about that man is true. He's obviously not going to be by himself. He's going to have a lot of hired thugs with him."

"Let the police handle it," Dave suggested.

"The police can't handle it," I replied. "As far as they're concerned, Cerney's clean. They don't have anything on him."

"You don't, either," Deseret said. "You don't know for sure if he's responsible for all that's happened here recently."

"That's where you're wrong. I do know. There was enough evidence in Reginald Masters's papers for me to know for sure."

"Most of which you haven't shared with the police," Dave said.

"I told you, they can't do anything."

Dave grumbled. "And you can. Brian Stratford, vigilante."

I was sitting upright now, and I was taking the offensive. "Hey, Cerney's unfinished business for me. He knows it, and he's not going to rest until he finishes me. I could give the police everything I've got and it wouldn't provide one ounce of protection for me or my friends. I don't have any hard evidence to convict him of anything, just gut instinct about what he intends to do about me. If I don't go after him, he's going to keep sending people after me. I'm not so afraid for myself, but I am afraid for all of you."

"You don't have to worry about us," Deseret said.

"Yes I do. That's one of the things that gives him an edge over me. He can keep sending people here, keep putting the heat on me without feeling any on himself. Well, I'm not going to let my life be like a Vietnam. I'm not going to just stay on this side of the Red River and play defense. I'll never again be put in a situation where I can't cross a line and the enemy can."

Dave, Betty and Deseret all seemed stunned by my sudden tirade.

"I'll tell you something else," I continued, "Cerney knows I'm coming. He's a man who studies his enemies. He knows me from the past, so he's aware of what to expect fro me. He'll be waiting, but when he has to deal with me in mountains and woodlands, in places where I don't have friends who can be hurt, then I have the advantage."

There was a hushed silence. I had revealed more of myself, shown more cold, calculating anger, then I had intended. In those brief minutes, they had all had a glimpse of who and what I had once been. And, possibly, what I might once again become.

I was in my office on Monday when the departmental secretary gave me a ring and told me I had a visitor. "It's a Mr. Bubba Ferris," she said.

I didn't have a clue as to who Bubba Ferris was, but told her to send him on back. Surprise! It was the guy I'd knocked through the window of the donut shop. He was standing there in my office doorway, cowboy hat in hand, looking sheepish.

"Mr. Stratford, I just wanted to come by to thank

you." he said.

His statement puzzled me. "Thank me? If you'll remember, I'm the one who knocked you through the window of the donut shop. I should be apologizing to you."

"No sir," he said. "I was way out of line and you gave me what I deserved."

"Well, have a seat Mr. Ferris and —"

He interrupted. "Call me Bubba. All my friends call me Bubba." He sat, but on the edge of the chair.

"Well, Bubba, there's really nothing you need to thank me for. I'd figure you'd want to kick my rear end."

"Naaaw," he slurred. "Besides, I'd be afraid I'd get mine kicked again. You're a pretty tough hombre, Mr. Stratford."

I laughed. "If I'm going to call you Bubba, then you need to call me Brian."

"Agreed. But what I'm here to thank you for is for not pressing charges against me."

"Since you didn't hit me, I'm not sure there would be any justification for me pressing charges. To tell the truth, you could probably have pressed charges against me."

It was his turn to laugh. "Man, was I drunk."

"You were that," I agreed.

There are some people whose names fit them perfectly. Bubba is such a person. He looks like a guy named Bubba is supposed to look. He lacks a good three inches being six feet tall, has a beer belly and a ruddy face that has seen more than its share of the sun. At first glance he looks a little soft, but there's an underlying Texas toughness to him that's a lot like old and worn leather.

"How old are you, Bubba?"

"I'm twenty-nine," was the answer.

"And what do you do?"

"I run a little barbecue place over in Oak Cliff." The reference was to a community in the southern portion of Dallas.

"I'll have to come by there sometime and sample your barbecue."

"It'll be on the house," he said.

"No need for that."

"Plenty of need for it," he disagreed. "And another thing. I went by and paid for the glass at the donut shop."

"You didn't have to do that. I was going to pay for it."

He grinned. "I'm the one who broke it."

Bubba was, I decided, a strange one. But I'd run into guys like him before, men who, if you battled them and won, became your lifelong friends. You have to whip them to earn their respect.

He stayed until I had to leave to teach a class, and I learned quite a bit about him. He had been a Navy diver and got into the barbecue business after serving a couple of hitches. His primary interest now was bass fishing. He had a twenty thousand dollar bass boat and a tricked out twenty thousand dollar Chevrolet Suburban with which to pull it. And he had a collection of guns that would be the envy of an army arsenal.

Just how much of Bubba was believable, I didn't know. And it really didn't matter. He was a nice enough fellow, and I was appreciative of the fact that he'd paid for the window.

After class, I drove to the bank, got the book out of my safety deposit box and made several copies of it. After putting the original back, I returned to my office and placed the copies with letters in envelopes addressed to the proper authorities. If something happened to me, the envelopes would be mailed and, hopefully, someone would pick up the mantle and carry on.

From shortly after discovering it, I'd kept a copy of the book on my person. I had studied it intently and was pretty sure I had cracked Cerney's code. Breaking codes is not one of my fields of expertise, but the Agency had helped me on it. I was relatively sure I knew how Cerney's operation functioned.

The names, of course, were dealers. But the coded material adjacent to each name indicated territory, normal delivery date and site for delivery, cost and type of product to the specific dealer, terms of sale and so on. Cerney had his drug operation set up like a successful chain store venture, and Reginald Masters had been his regional manager.

Later in the afternoon Dave came by and said, "Betty and I would like to take you and Deseret out to dinner tomorrow night."

"I don't think so."

"Why not?"

"Well, under the circumstances, I think it best that I not see Deseret socially."

Tongue-in-cheek he asked, "Is it because you're going to be killed this weekend?"

I laughed. "I'm not going to be killed."

"I would bet on that, but you're the only one who'd

cover and you won't be around for me to collect from."

"Seriously, Dave, from the beginning I've had some real reservations about seeing Deseret socially. It's more than just the age thing, too. It's my financial status...a lot of things."

He countered. "You're crazy. You may have a high IQ, but you sure as hell don't have any common sense."

I chuckled at his commentary. "Thanks a lot. Since you're supposed to be my best friend, that tells me a lot about what other people think of me."

"Since when have you cared what anyone thought about you?" he asked. "Frankly, Brian, you can be a pompous, self-righteous ass at times, a real holier-than-thou jerk. Deseret's the best thing that ever happened to you, and you're determined to screw it up."

My laugh was uneasy. Dave had never been one to get on my case, about anything. "I thought you and Betty were opposed to Deseret. At least where I'm concerned."

"We were at first, but we've gotten to know her. We probably know her a lot better than you do. She and Betty have spent quite a bit of time together. They've become good friends."

"Well, the situation —"

He interrupted. "I don't want to hear it, Brian. Do you want to go tomorrow night or not?"

"I'll go, but it's against my best judgment."

He sighed. "I wouldn't have it any other way."

It was after he left that I realized Dave had intimidated me into doing what he wanted. It was hard to believe I had allowed it. But of late, a lot of things were hard to believe.

16

On Tuesday evening, Dave and Betty picked me up at my apartment. "Deseret will just meet us there," Betty explained. Betty had taken it on herself to ask Dez to join us for dinner.

"Where are we going?" I asked.

"It's a surprise," Dave said.

I was feeling a bit subdued, so I didn't pursue the matter. However, when Dave headed the car south of downtown Dallas on Interstate Thirty-Five, I again asked, "Where in the hell are we going?"

"To Oak Cliff," was Dave's reply.

"Fine," I grumbled.

"You sure are grumpy tonight," Betty said.

Dave opined, "I can't see much difference in him. He's always grumpy."

"Just keep it up," I said. "I know all this is amusing to you two."

"That's where you're wrong," Betty said. "We don't enjoy watching a friend make a fool of himself."

"Until now, I wasn't aware that I was making a fool of myself."

"You are where Dez is concerned," she said. "Believe me, she's mature enough to handle the age difference. And money's not that important to her."

"Money's never important if you have a lot of it."

Betty laughed. "You're impossible. What she sees in you, what any woman could see in you, baffles me."

"C'mon, Betty, if Dave weren't around, you'd be camping on my doorstep," I jokingly said.

"Brother," she said, slurring the word. "If this joker ever dumped me, I sure wouldn't go after any of his friends, especially you. He's never had very good taste in friends."

"Betty, Betty," Dave said in a mock-chiding tone, "you might be on the verge of doing terrible damage to Brian's ego."

"Fat chance," she replied.

The bantering went on until Dave parked the car in front of a nondescript building with a sign reading,

BUBBA'S BAR-B-Q.

"Why this place?" I asked.

"Isn't Bubba a friend of yours?" Dave asked.

"Hell, I hardly know the man. I only met him yesterday. He's the guy I knocked through the plate glass window at the donut shop."

"I'll be damned," Dave said. "He talked to me yesterday, invited the whole journalism faculty and all your friends out here for a surprise party for you."

"The man doesn't know any of my friends, not that I have that many."

Dave sheepishly said, "He gave me the job of inviting all your friends."

I started chuckling. "With all that's happened lately, why shouldn't a guy I talked to for maybe fifteen minutes throw me a surprise party? Hell, let's go in and enjoy ourselves."

On entering the place, Bubba greeted me like I was his dearest friend, someone he had known forever. He ushered us over to a group of tables that had been shoved together to form one long platform. Dez, Alan and Honey were seated at the table, along with other members of the journalism faculty.

After greetings were exchanged, I took a chair between Dez and Honey. Several persons at the table were sucking on longneck bottles of Lone Star Beer, others had glasses of wine.

"What's the occasion?" Alan wanted to know. "Is it your birthday or something?"

"To my knowledge, there is no occasion," I answered. "I have no idea why I'm here."

"Your friend Bubba seems to be a nice fellow," Alan said.

"Yeah, he's okay," I agreed. I figured it was pointless to try to explain my relationship to Bubba. I'd decided it would be best to just go with the flow.

Deseret smiled and said, "Kind of different isn't it."

I laughed. "Definitely not the kind of place where I'd expect to see you and your parents. The wine isn't half bad, though, which surprises me."

"Don't be too surprised. Bubba called daddy and asked him what kind he should buy. By the way, I can't recall you ever mentioning Bubba. Have you been friends long?"

"To tell the truth, Dez —"

Bubba interrupted. "You folks have everything you need?"

"Yeah, Bubba," I answered, "we're fine. You've really outdone yourself this time."

Speaking to Deseret and referring to me, he said, "This guy's okay. He's one tough dude."

"I agree about him being okay," Deseret said.

Bubba slapped me on the back and went back to doing whatever a person does who runs a barbecue place. I was going to continue telling Deseret about Bubba, but Lightfoot came up and introduced his wife to us.

"Good party," he commented.

"A real surprise," I said.

He laughed. "I imagine so. You seem to have a knack for the strange."

The barbecue and side dishes were excellent. I suspected the beef, ribs, and chicken were better than what Bubba served to his normal clientele. However, when I suggested the possibility to him, he denied it and said, "Serve the best barbecue and the world will beat a path to your door." I would learn that Bubba is a master of clichés.

As the evening wore on and the wine, beer, and barbecue sauce began to take effect, I couldn't help but notice Dave engaged in separate secretive and obviously serious conversations with Alan, Bubba and Lightfoot. It bothered me because...well, if Dave were in charge of national defense, the Russians could learn everything they ever wanted to know about us by just serving him a few glasses of wine.

My contemplation about Dave was interrupted by Honey, who said, "You know, I've never been in a place like this before. And I guess I've never really eaten good barbecue, because I like this."

Deseret responded, "Mother, if you'd get out of the house more often, and out of that little circle of friends you have, there's no telling what you might discover."

Alan laughed. "Maybe I ought to do the same. It's easy to get in a rut in terms of places to go and friends. I'd forgotten people like Bubba existed. Maybe I never even knew."

Earlier I'd asked Bubba why his girlfriend hadn't attended the party. He told us she was working, proudly announced that she danced at a topless joint just off McKinney Avenue.

"If y'all want to, we can go over there after we get through here," he said.

I tried to beg off, but Alan, Honey, Deseret, Dave, and Betty insisted we go. Since I was dependent on Dave for a ride, their wishes derailed me.

"I've never been to a topless club," Honey said.

I came back, "There's no point in getting a complete education in one night."

"I've never been to one, either," Betty said.

"Neither have I," Deseret chimed in.

Dave started to say something, but I suggested, "I wouldn't."

Therefore, at a little after eleven o'clock, we were in the club where Bubba's lady, Chi Chi Knockers, was plying her trade.

"That's her stage name, not her real name," Bubba

explained. "Her real name's Bernice Sue Smith."

"I wonder why she chose the name Chi Chi Knockers?" Honey asked.

Fortunately, a well-endowed waitress came to take our drink order before the question could be answered. She was topless, too, prompting Bubba to explain, "The girls all dance and waitress."

The place wasn't all that crowded and, of course, the clientele was mostly male. There were a few women customers, some of whom I suspected were hookers. Deseret, Betty, and Honey were being thoroughly scrutinized by all the eyes in the place.

"It's different," Deseret whispered to me. "Do you come to these places often?"

I gave her an incredulous look, then whispered, "I never come to these places. If you'll recall, coming here tonight wasn't my idea."

When Chi Chi came on stage to do her number, there wasn't any doubt as to why she had chosen the name Knockers. Possibly because of the way she was dressed, I hadn't noticed that night at the donut shop. But after seeing her on stage, I decided she probably had to have specially made bras.

"Ain't she something?" Bubba said.

"She sure is," I agreed.

After her bump and grind routine was completed, Chi Chi put on a mesh jacket that didn't hide anything and joined us at our table. I expected Deseret, Betty, and Honey to be a little snobbish toward her, but they, instead, seemed genuinely fascinated. They asked her all kinds of questions, resulting in the drinking and conversation lasting well past midnight.

I finally got home about one-thirty.

Wednesday morning broke cool and clear, but the anticipation of a beautiful day was not enough to offset a terrible headache and the feeling that strange little people were doing a reconstruction job on the inside of my stomach. It was enough to make me consider the possibility that wine and barbecue are not compatible.

I downed a couple of Extra Strength Excedrin, then drove to a convenience store and bought a bottle of Pepto-Bismol. I took a gulp of the pink liquid straight from the bottle.

Though food was the last thing I wanted, I'm a creature of habit. So I ended up at the small cafe near the university where I always have breakfast. There I ordered a bowl of grits and coffee.

It was seven o'clock.

I had just started on the grits when Lightfoot came in and seated himself at my booth.

"I thought I'd find you here," he said. In our previous conversations, I'd told him where he could usually find me early in the morning.

"Don't talk too loud, Mark, my head is killing me."

He laughed. "That was quite a party last night."

"It sure was," I agreed.

The waitress came to the booth and he asked her to duplicate my order.

"I've been doing a little checking on your friend Bubba —"

I interrupted, "Damn it, I hardly know the man."

He laughed again. "Don't get your rear in an uproar.

The guy has obviously decided you're his friend."

I sighed. "That I can't help."

"Well, I'll say this. He serves some mean barbecue."

"Your stomach in bad shape, too."

"No, I'm saying it was good. Maybe the best I've ever eaten. Sorry the wife and I couldn't go with you to the topless place, but it might not look too good for me to be in a place like that."

"Hell, it didn't look good for me to be there. But you're saying the barbecue didn't do anything to your stomach?"

"That's right, but I drank beer with mine. I can't believe you'd drink wine with barbecue."

"This morning, I can't believe I did it, either. But what about ol' Bubba?"

"From what I've been able to find out, he's straight arrow," Lightfoot said. "Of course, he *has* been arrested a few times for being drunk and disorderly, and also for aggravated assault."

"My kind of guy," I said. "Any particular reason why you ran a check on him?"

"Are you kidding? With all that's happened to you lately, I'd check out your mother if she came in contact with you."

"The hood who's still alive, the one who was helping hold the Antareses as hostages, and the one who was watching my apartment, have you gotten anything from them yet?"

"They're both still in the hospital. You're not the gentlest man I know in dealing with the criminal element."

I chuckled. "They won't talk anyway, not unless they're

properly tortured."

"Properly tortured? What in the hell does that mean?"

"Oh, nothing in particular. Chances are that you could torture those two guys to death and they wouldn't say anything."

"I know this may come as a shock to you, Brian, but we don't torture prisoners."

I grunted. "I know that, Mark. I'm not even suggesting it, just making a comment."

"But I'll bet you wouldn't object if I left one of them alone with you in a room."

I grinned. "It might be a shortcut to getting a little information.

"Bubba might be a shortcut, too," he said.

"What do you mean?"

"Well, ol' Bubba might be straight, but he knows some people who aren't."

"Drug dealers?"

"That topless joint where his girl works, there are times when drugs change hands in that place," Lightfoot said.

"So, why haven't the police done anything about it?"

"Oh, it's been hit a few times, but the only ones caught in the backwash so far have been a few junkies. We can't seem to get a handle on any of the major dealers."

"And you think Bubba may know some of them?"

"Maybe. I don't think he's a user, but he probably knows some junkies who might be able to give us a line."

"And you obviously want me to work ol' Bubba for you."

"The thought occurred to me."

"What makes you think Bubba knows anything or

anybody?"

"His known associates," Lightfoot said. "Don't ask me to give you any names because you know I can't do that."

"I wasn't going to ask. I know you have to protect your sources."

"So, do you want to take a run at Bubba?"

"I'll give it some thought."

"Maybe he's heard of Cerney."

"I doubt it. Cerney's a man who covers his tracks well."

"If what you say about him is true, he must," Lightfoot agreed. "We don't have a thing on him."

Back at my office I gave serious thought to what my detective friend had asked me to do. I figured I didn't have a thing to lose, so I gave Bubba a call.

When he answered, I said, "First, Bubba, I want to thank you for the party last night. I think everyone had a great time."

"They couldn't have had any better time than I did," he said. "Your friends are real nice people."

"Yeah, they are," I agreed. "But I was wondering if we could get together for a cup of coffee this morning."

"Sure. What time?"

"Well, I have class until nine-fifty, and it'll take me a while to get out there."

"Why don't I just come over there?"

"That would be too much trouble for you."

"Naw, it's no trouble. I just need to get back in time to handle the lunch traffic."

I argued against him making the trip, but he insisted. We agreed to meet at the small restaurant where I'd had breakfast.

By the time I arrived there, almost ten on the nose, Bubba was already entrenched in a booth with a cup of coffee in front of him. I sat and ordered the same.

With Bubba, I figured the direct approach was best. "The police think you may have a line on some drug connections. I've been asked to talk to you, to see if you can provide some names."

Bubba chuckled. "Brian, I like the way you come right to the point."

"I didn't see any reason to beat around the bush."

"There's not any," he said. "There are some things you ought to know about me, one being that I hate dopers. Of course, cops aren't on my list of favorite people, either. They've hassled me lots of times when it wasn't necessary."

"From what I understand, you've had a little trouble controlling your liquor."

He grunted. "Yeah, that's true. And if you'd pressed charges against me, Brian, I might be in jail today."

"Like I told you before, there wasn't any reason to."

"Regardless, I appreciate what you did. And if you want the names of some junkies, I guess I can get them for you."

"I don't want you to do anything you're not comfortable doing," I said. "And I'm not so much interested in the junkies as I am in the suppliers."

"I'm not saying I know any," he said, "but I might know some people who do."

"Have you ever heard the name Foster Cerney?"

"I can't say that I have," he replied.

Maybe it was his willingness to help that caused me to

do so, I'm not sure, but I found myself telling Bubba about Cerney and my relationship to him. After I'd finished, he said, "It sounds to me like you're a man with a mission, Brian. Frankly, I wouldn't want to be in Cerney's shoes."

"All I can give the police right now is speculation, which they're not that interested in," I admitted. "If I could just get a line on one of his dealers, maybe I could furnish them a little proof."

The book, of course, contained names, which I initially thought were names of dealers. However, in investigating, I discovered that even the names were a code.

"I'll sniff around a bit, Brian, and get back to you. Maybe as early as this afternoon."

"I'd appreciate it."

"I just want you to know I'll do this for you, but I'm not doing it for the cops."

The afternoon was pretty well taken up by the routine. Deseret did, however, come by around three-thirty and asked if I'd like to make a happy hour somewhere.

"After last night, I've given up drinking," I told her. "From now on it's strictly Pepto-Bismol straight up."

She laughed. "The evening didn't seem to affect anyone else. You must have a sensitive stomach."

"I don't know. I just know I've been in pain most of the day."

"Well, I need to go to the library anyway," she said.

I went home about five, and had been puttering around the place for about an hour when the doorbell rang.

It was Deseret.

"Since your stomach is in such pain," she said, "I thought I'd bring you something that would go easy on it."

She came in, set a couple of blueberry sundaes on the dining table.

"It's so bad," I moaned in a joking manner, "that I'm not sure I can even eat ice cream."

"If you can't eat ice cream, I'm taking you to the hospital," she said with a laugh.

Deseret looked more delicious than the sundae, but it was good and it soothed some of the creaking and groaning in my stomach. After we finished the sundaes, we went into what serves as a living room and sat on the couch.

"You know, I can't believe mom and dad," she said.

"What do you mean?"

"I'm talking about how much they enjoyed last night. It's hard to believe, my mother and father in a topless place."

"It's just as hard for me to imagine them at Bubba's place," I said.

She laughed. "Yeah, that's hard to believe, too."

She looked so beautiful in the soft glow of lamplight, so desirable. When I looked deeply into her eyes, the world just sort of dissolved around me. Before I even realized it, she was in my arms and I was kissing her passionately. All my resolve, all my reasons for not allowing Deseret to become the most important thing in my life, were swept away.

What might have happened if we hadn't been interrupted, I'm not sure. But the harsh ringing of the telephone broke the mood.

"Do you have to get that?" she asked.

"I'd better."

The caller was Bubba.

"Meet me at Rockwall Marina in an hour," he said.

"I'll be there." That was the extent of the conversation. The marina, on Lake Ray Hubbard, is about a forty-five minute drive from my apartment.

"That was quick," Deseret commented.

"It was Bubba. He wants me to meet him at Rockwall Marina."

"Mind if I tag along?" she asked.

I kissed her, then said, "I'd enjoy your company."

"When do you have to be there?"

"In an hour, so we'll have to leave right away."

"Too bad. Why don't you let me drive you, since you must be in pain from that bad stomach?"

"Funny," I said with a laugh, "something made me forget all about my pain. But I don't think my stomach's the reason you want to drive. You just don't like to ride in the Ramcharger."

"It's bumpy."

"Then you drive," I said. Before we left, I put on my shoulder holster carrying the nine millimeter automatic. With my jacket on, no one could tell I was carrying a gun.

As we were driving toward the Lake, Deseret asked, "Do you mind letting me in on what Bubba wants?"

I hesitated, then said, "Not at all." I then told her I had solicited Bubba's help in getting a lead on a dope dealer.

"I wish there was some way you could let this go," she said, "but I know you can't."

"If I could let it go, Dez, if I could turn Cerney over to someone else, I would. He thinks I know something, so I've become a target. If he wasn't occupied with something more important, he would have had me nailed by now."

"God knows, he's tried."

"He's made some attempts to get the book, but those attempts were nothing compared to what he's capable of. And if he had gotten the book, I'd be dead by now."

"I don't like to hear you talk like that."

"Sorry, but I'm a realist. If someone like Cerney decides they want me dead, there's not much I can do to prevent it. I might take a few guys with me, but eventually the numbers decide the game."

"Game," she said incredulously, "do you think it's all a game?"

"Poor choice of words. Whatever it is, there's no one who can't be hit."

She was silent for a few moments, then said, "You know, I guess maybe I thought it was a game at first, but then those people came to the house and —"

I interrupted. "I know, baby, and I'd give anything to have kept you and your family out of this. At the time, though, I had no idea of all that was involved."

"There was no way you could have known," she said. "And as for keeping us out of it, it might have been the best thing that ever happened to us."

I laughed. "I sure don't understand your logic."

"Well, it sort of revitalized mom and dad. They were in a rut, not enjoying life all that much. But since you came into our lives, there has been some adventure."

"Frankly, I could do with a little less adventure," I said.

"You really don't understand, do you?"

"I guess not."

"Maybe I can explain it, I'm not sure. Dad's always been an office person and mom's always been a housewife. They've had the same little circle of friends for years. They do the same things, they talk about the same things. Until recently, dad's biggest adventure was getting to play eighteen holes of golf some place in Scotland. Mom's biggest deal was to be chairperson of some charity ball. We've traveled a little as a family, but everything we've done has been like following a boring script."

"There's a lot to be said for security," I said. "I'm sure there are lots of people who would enjoy being part of that boring Antares family script."

She then delivered a verbal jab, "The money bothers you, doesn't it?"

"Maybe. Yeah, I guess it does."

"You can't buy happiness with money."

I chuckled. "I've heard that all my life, but I've never had a chance to run any tests."

"Well, take my word for it."

"Dez, I can tell you that poverty or lack of money doesn't assure happiness, either. I mean, hell, look at you. You're wearing a pant suit that probably cost five hundred dollars, a mink jacket and diamond ring that cost thousands. I won't even guess what you pay for a pair of shoes. Can you honestly tell me that you'd be happier in rags?"

She laughed. "Well, no. But I could be happy with you with a lot less than I have now. After all, what's really important, Brian?"

"Maybe you'd better tell me. What do you really want out of life, Dez?"

"I want a man who loves me more than anything else in the world, a decent home and children. And I think I'd like a degree of security. My real idea of security is a husband who loves me more than anything else in the world."

As far as I was concerned, Deseret's summation pretty well took care of all the important things in life. I guess that's when I started thinking of her as more than just a girl with a beautiful face and body. From early on I had recognized her superior intellect. Now I was beginning to see the substance, the depth, of which Betty had spoken.

As for me, I could see myself in the role of the loving husband, although I had previously failed in that department. But as for children, I had some doubts along those lines. Regardless, overall I couldn't see myself spending the rest of my life in a nice little house with a wife and kids, even though the sound of the idea was appealing.

"Hopefully, you'll get what you want out of life, Dez."

"Hopefully," she said.

17

Bubba was already at Rockwall Marina when we arrived.

"I didn't know you were going to bring your girlfriend," he said. "We need to go out on the water and it's probably going to be cold. It might be dangerous, too."

"Do you mind waiting here?" I asked Deseret.

"I most certainly do," she said.

Bubba laughed. "It's going to be a lot warmer here than on the water. If you don't mind my saying so, you're not exactly dressed for a boat ride."

"Don't worry about me," she said. "I'll be plenty warm."

"How long do you think we'll be out?" I asked.

Bubba shrugged his shoulders. "Could be three or four hours."

"You'd better call your folks," I told Deseret. She didn't balk at the suggestion, went inside the marina office to use the telephone.

"How much can I say around her?" Bubba asked.

"She's okay. You can say anything you like. With her

along, I would like to avoid anything dangerous."

"I think we'll be okay," he said. "There is going to be a drop tonight, but we can watch it from a distance."

"You mean the drop is going to be on the lake?"

"If my sources are right. You know that Cerney guy you asked me about?"

"Yeah."

"These are his people."

When Deseret came out of the marina office, we walked to the slip where Bubba had his Stratos bass boat. A big one hundred fifty horsepower Mercury outboard was perched on its tail.

In the boat, Bubba provided us with life jackets, then cranked the engine. Once we were clear of the marina, he yelled "hang on" and pushed the throttle forward. The boat lurched forward and we were immediately skimming across the surface of the water.

"How fast will this thing run?" I asked.

"It'll do close to eighty," Bubba replied.

I'm not sure how far we went or what route we took. I just know that after leaving Rockwall Marina, Bubba took the boat under a bridge on Interstate Thirty and headed west. After a time he cut back under another Interstate Thirty bridge and headed north, into an area where trees were sticking up out of the water like unwakened ghosts. Maybe they wouldn't have struck me that way in daylight, but with a kind of steamy mist rising just off the water's surface, the place was downright eerie.

Bubba had cut the engine down to where the boat was just crawling through the timber. Occasionally, we'd bump an underwater stump or log. Finally, he cut the engine, went to the bow of the boat and dropped a foot-operated electric troll motor in the water. He used the electric motor to get us in position, then shut it off, pulled it back up into its bracket and clamped it down.

"The drop's supposed to be in that area," he half whispered, pointing to a large opening off the trees. "I don't think we can be seen back here."

"We should be okay," I agreed.

"Bubba, just in case we are seen, do you have any firepower?" Deseret said.

"Firepower? What's this firepower stuff coming out of your mouth?" I asked.

Bubba chuckled softly. "Looks like your little lady's getting ready for combat."

Deseret grumbled. "I'd appreciate it if you'd talk to me, Bubba, not talk about me to Brian."

"Whew! I didn't mean to pull your string. She's kind of fiesty, ain't she."

I shrugged my shoulders and jokingly said, "She does have a streak of meanness in her. If I were you, I'd do what she asks."

"Oh, I intend to," Bubba assured. "But in answer to your question, look in that rod box and you'll find just about anything we'll need."

I opened the rod box and was surprised by its contents.

"Hell, you even have a night scope on one of these rifles," I said. "Where did you get it?"

"I bought it," he replied. "The damn thing cost me over five thousand dollars."

I was quite familiar with the scope Bubba had on the rifle. We had used them in 'Nam. With one, you can spot an enemy lurking among trees or other cover on the darkest of nights. To me, the scope represents the ultimate in technology for a foot soldier.

"I don't think we'll need it tonight," I said.

My reasoning was based on the brightness of the moon, its soft rays caressing the rippling water.

"You're right," Bubba said. "Give Deseret and me shotguns. You take the automatic weapon."

"Do you have a permit for this thing?" I asked while checking the automatic.

Bubba chuckled. "Of course I do. You wouldn't expect ol' Bubba to do something illegal, would you?"

Dez said, "You know, Brian, it would be romantic out here in the moonlight if we weren't sitting here with guns waiting to spy on people."

"Hey, it's romantic with you anyway, anywhere."

"Sorry, you two," Bubba said, "if there was someplace I could go right now so the two of you could be alone, I'd go."

Deseret laughed. "Never mind, Bubba, he's all talk."

"Nice shot," Bubba said with a chuckle. Before I could counter, he continued, "I'm going to pull us a little closer to the edge of the clearing."

Grabbing trees with his hands and pulling, Bubba started the big boat forward. I tried to help. It was as we were pulling the boat between two large trees that we saw the body. Deseret swallowed a shriek of horror, and both Bubba and I were so startled our legs shoved us backwards.

"My god!" Bubba exclaimed.

The man had been hung, the rope tied to a limb on one

of the big trees. Even in the moonlight, the grotesque, surprised look on the face of the man was easy to see.

"It's the guy who told me about the drop," Bubba said.

Even before he could get all the words out of his mouth, I heard a familiar sound, one that had been all too familiar in 'Nam. Then the helicopter rose like some giant creature, unreal in appearance. It was suddenly just there, above the trees and in front of us.

Just as suddenly, we were bathed in the rays of a spotlight, and another all too familiar sound occurred. Bullets were plunking in the water all around us.

By then I had the automatic weapon trained on the chopper and unloaded a few rounds. The burst took out the spotlight. Bubba and Deseret were busy blasting away with their shotguns.

The helicopter pulled up and away, but I figured it would be back.

"Let's get the hell out of here," I yelled at Bubba.

He was already at the boat's controls, cranking the engine, pushing the throttle and crashing through the mostly dead timber. The engine whined and groaned, but it didn't quit. When the boat hit the clearing, Bubba let the hammer down and we went roaring across the surface.

For a few brief moments I thought we might be all right, but then I saw the big ugly bird making a fast approach. I knew the chopper's pilot would try to get alongside us so his shooter would have a better angle, so I tried to dissuade him with a few more bursts from my weapon.

Deseret was positioned beside me, firing her shotgun. I

was proud of her, too proud to tell her the chopper was too far away for the shotgun to do any damage. For some reason I wanted to pull her to me and kiss her right then, but timing is everything; and with the chopper's maneuverability, we didn't have much time.

We were rapidly approaching Interstate Thirty and one of its bridges, so I tugged on Bubba's sleeve and yelled, "Stop this baby under the bridge."

He nodded acknowledgment and I fired a few more bursts at the chopper. The pilot pulled his ship up and away. His action enabled Bubba to slow down enough to stop the boat under the bridge and position it between some pilings.

"Dez, you and Bubba get down in the bottom of the boat and I'll try to nail him when he comes down looking for us."

Her teeth were clenched and she had a defiant look, her shotgun at the ready position. "No way," she said.

Bubba laughed. "I'm with her. I want to get a shot, too."

There was no need, no time to argue. If the pilot brought the chopper down to look for us under the bridge, it would be almost a sitting duck. But then, so were we. It would probably be a matter of who fired first.

Suddenly the chopper was there, on the north side of the bridge, its side toward us. We all fired simultaneously and I saw the gunner lurch back from his position at the open door. The pilot also caught a burst, and the helicopter just seemed to nose into the water.

"Yahoo!" Bubba yelled.

Deseret was equally excited. "We did it," she screamed.

"We did it."

We had, indeed, done it.

"You have to be the luckiest crazy man I know," Lightfoot said. "I don't know why you refuse to call me when you think something's going down."

"Hell, I didn't know anything was going down. Bubba asked me to meet him at the lake, I go, and the first thing I know I'm in a boat, a dead man is hanging from a tree and some guys in a helicopter are using us for target practice."

Lightfoot laughed. "Some people would think a scenario like that could only be on television, but it's getting to be old hat with you, isn't it?"

I grunted. "You know Bubba is certifiably crazy, don't you?"

"Hey, he's your pal," the detective said. "And I think you've got one you're not going to be able to get rid of."

I groaned. "Why me?"

"Do you want to hear about your two latest victims?"

"If you're talking about the two guys in the chopper, I can already tell you that they probably didn't have any identification and that they were probably Vietnamese."

Lightfoot chuckled. "If we ever have a police quiz show, you'd be one helluva contestant."

"What about the chopper? Someone had to own it."

"Someone did, but —"

I interrupted, "Unfortunately, he's dead."

"Bingo," Lightfoot said. "He was also an oriental, and

he was killed in an auto accident a couple of years ago."

"Maintenance, what about maintenance?" I asked. "Oh, hell. It stands to reason that Cerney would have his own maintenance people."

"We certainly haven't got a line on any maintenance work being done on it around here," the detective said. "We're running some checks in Oklahoma, but I doubt that we'll find anything."

"And no flight plans or anything like that?"

"Dream on."

"Did Bubba tell you anything about the guy who was hanged?"

"Are you kidding?" Lightfoot asked. "The man won't give us the time of day."

"Well, he's not real fond of cops."

"You're becoming a master of understatement. Fortunately, we're familiar with the guy who was hanged. He's local, did a little dealing, but nothing major. I doubt that Bubba knew him any better than we did."

"Well, I appreciate the fact that you didn't overdo it on interrogating us. You could have made it a lot tougher."

Lightfoot had taken our statements on the lake incident without hassle, and without a lot of unnecessary questions.

"My superiors would be all over me if I made things tough on the Three Musketeers," Lightfoot said jokingly. "They're anxious for you to get out on the streets again to see what else you can stir up. They enjoy hearing about a little ruckus now and then."

I gave him my best bemused look. "Now don't you go joshing me, Mr. Lightfoot."

"Seriously, I think a few folks around here are beginning to believe what you said about Masters and the Beckers not being suicides," the detective said. "God knows, we're all aware of the drug problem in Dallas. We have almost as many junkies as queers."

I laughed. "I didn't know it was that bad."

"Of course, we've got a lot of queer junkies," he said. "You know, Brian, I've never understood why the city council is so damned patronizing to the gays."

"It's bad humor," I concluded, "but politics makes strange bedfellows. The gays have become a political force."

He chuckled, then said, "All I know is that dope and AIDS are enough to keep us all dodging. And it's getting worse, not better."

"How in the hell did you get the conversation off on queers?"

"I dunno. I guess it's because I think of them as being as much a disease as drug dealers."

"I agree, for all the hell good it's going to do."

It was easy enough to sympathize with Lightfoot regarding drug trafficking in Dallas. It's a city on the move, growing in population and problems. No one seems to have any answers to the problems. Hell, no one even asks any questions anymore, not the media, not anybody. There's just a lot of acceptance of the powers that be, powers whose voices are raised most often for their own benefit and not the city's.

There's been a lot of flight to the suburbs to avoid the problems. But parents can't be faulted for trying to eliminate problems for their kids. There are enough problems with adolescence without adding unnecessary ones.

Lightfoot hates drug dealers as much as I do, but for them to survive there has to be a market. And the Dallas area is one of the best. It is not just the dregs of society who are hooked on the habit, either. It permeates every social and economic strata.

"How did Deseret handle the deal last night?" Lightfoot asked. "I'm talking about emotionally."

"Surprisingly well. I am worried about her, though. She hasn't really talked about the guy she nailed at their house. I know it was a kill or be killed situation, but I'm sure the fact that she killed him is gnawing away at her insides."

Lightfoot grunted. "After last night, she may have two notches on her gun."

"It's hard to say whether she did any damage with the shotgun or not, but shooting at the same target everyone else is shooting at and not knowing whether you hit it has to be easier on her than blasting someone at pointblank range."

"How did you feel the first time you blew someone away?" Lightfoot asked.

"I don't remember. Oh, hell, that's a lie. I was sick to my stomach and threw up all over myself. But where I was, I didn't have much time to grieve."

Lightfoot laughed. "Well, Deseret's just too much of a lady to throw up in public. With all that's been going on, she hasn't had all that much time to think about the shooting."

"You're probably right," I agreed. "I'll tell you this

about her, she'll do to ride shotgun for you."

"I'd say you have a couple there, Deseret and Bubba, who a man wouldn't mind having beside him in a fight."

"Early on, I sure misjudged her," I said.

"Just because you're a college professor," the detective said with a chuckle, "doesn't mean you're necessarily bright."

18

Deseret was experiencing emotional trauma, but not from the shooting alone. There were a lot of other things, such as her relationship with Brian.

She had come clean, told him why she had initially made contact with him. If her confession bothered him, he hadn't let it show. He had simply said, "The way things are now, I don't guess it really matters how we met or why."

He was always so damn noncommital, so cool and reserved. She wished that just once he'd crush her in his arms, kiss her with all the pent-up passion in his soul, be totally out of control.

But he won't, she grumbled to herself. He treats me like I'm some kind of fragile doll, like it'll break me if he isn't careful.

Since her parents had backed off, more or less given their blessing to the relationship with Brian, she had been having some doubts. It wasn't a matter of loving him. She was sure she did. Or, at least, as sure as she was capable of being. A lifetime relationship, though, that merited some serious thinking. She realized she might soon have to deal with things that initially hadn't seemed important, things she had shoved to the back of her mind.

Of course, Brian hadn't talked of marriage. He would, eventually. She mentally chuckled, thinking if he didn't she would be one teed-off female. That's the part she didn't understand, the contradictory thinking going off like fireworks in her mind.

On the one hand, she wanted Brian to ask her to marry him. On the other, she hoped he wouldn't. At least, not now.

Maybe I'm getting the cart ahead of the horse, she thought. The man never even tells me he loves me. And here I am afraid he'll ask me to marry him.

Again, she told herself, the fear had nothing to do with her love for him. It was just that maybe it was too soon. After all, they had known each other for only a short time. That hadn't seemed important during the first stages of their romance, but now . . .

And the age difference, which she didn't at first see as a problem, could be . . . The problem was, she thought, that he often treated her like a child. Because she wasn't, she resented being treated as such.

There was also the problem of his children. In terms of age, she was separated from them by only a few years. How would they react to her? How would they feel about her? How did she herself feel about inheriting an already existing family?

There was Brian's past — how much about that should she know? She had never been in many crisis situations, but she was sure he reacted differently to them than most persons would. In the recent life threatening situations in which she had been involved, he had maintained an almost frightening cool and seeming disregard for his own life. He had seemed totally in control.

There had, of course, been the rumors floating around campus regarding his past. The talk had made him seem exciting, mysterious, and romantic, like someone out of a spy novel. But the rumors, the talk, had been somewhat mystical, making Brian's past world a million light years away from the security of the campus.

Now that security had been breached by his past, by his unwillingness to accept things as they seemed. Not that she wanted him to walk away from the murders of the dean and the Beckers, or from trying to bring down a major dope dealer. She just wished he would trust and enlist the aid of others to help him.

Was killing easy for him? He hadn't talked about it, and the only persons she knew he had killed or injured were those who had sought to do bodily harm to him. Or to her and her parents. She suspected, however, that he wasn't a virgin when it came to killing.

It had all seemed fine as long as it was talk or rumor. Then it was like a western movie where when a white hat killed a black hat, the audience felt elation. But when you were witness to even a black hat being killed, any joy was momentary and the death not that easy to forget.

In her mind, in her dreams, she kept seeing the face of the man she had shot on Saturday night. He was there at the window, then the bullets were hitting him and he was gone. She feared the dream, the mental image, would never go away. That it would be with her forever.

She shuddered now in thinking about it. She had wanted to talk to Brian about it, but couldn't. She didn't think he would understand.

It was Thursday, midmorning. And following Wednesday night's harrowing experience, she had decided to cut her classes. It wasn't because she wanted to sleep in. Lately, sleep had become a difficult task.

She worried about Brian, knowing that on Friday morning he would be leaving for Oklahoma for a possible confrontation with Foster Cerney. She knew it wouldn't do any good to suggest that he solicit help, and he had let her know in no uncertain terms that she couldn't go on the trip. But she had determined to do something to help him, no matter what he said.

With all I'm worrying about, she thought, I need a diversion. I'll call Betty, see if she wants to meet me at the North Park Mall. Maybe if I buy something, I'll feel better.

She thought about a bumper sticker she had recently seen, WHEN THE GOING GETS TOUGH, THE TOUGH GO SHOPPING. *My kind of bumper sticker, she thought.*

When she called Betty and suggested lunch and a shopping trip, she found a willing soulmate. They agreed to meet at Houston's Restaurant on Walnut Hill, then go to the mall.

Deseret arrived at Houston's at eleven-thirty, about five minutes before Betty got there. They were seated at a table, ordered drinks and began scanning the menu.

"What have you been up to?" Betty asked.

"I guess you heard about last night," Deseret replied.

"No, I haven't heard anything."

Deseret proceeded to tell Betty all that had occurred the night before, causing her to proclaim, "That damn

Brian is going to get you killed."

With a chuckle, Deseret said, "Well, there were a few times last night when I thought we didn't have a prayer. But that Brian, he's cool as a cucumber. Bubba, he's just crazy as a loon."

Betty grumbled. "I can't believe Brian would expose you to danger like that."

"Oh, I don't think it was intentional. I don't think he would have let me to to the lake with him if he had thought there was any more to it than Bubba just giving him some information."

"I just don't know what's going on," Betty said. "Ever since this semester started, we've had all kinds of strange happenings. And it hasn't been just the dean's and the Becker deaths, either. I hate to say it, but I think things would be a lot more peaceful if it weren't for Brian."

"It's not his fault that someone killed the dean and the Beckers," Deseret replied defensively.

"No, but what about you and your parents being taken as hostages? That was sure a matter of Brian's past catching up with him."

"Maybe. But if I hadn't stuck my nose in Brian's life, it wouldn't have happened."

Betty laughed. "That's true. Dave and I might have been the ones taken hostage if it wasn't for you."

A waiter interrupted their conversation to take their order. After he left the table, Betty continued, "Don't take me wrong, Dez, Dave and I love Brian, even if he does get on my nerves sometimes."

"How does he get on your nerves?"

"For one thing, his indecision about you. I think he's

crazy about you, but it might be a cold day in hell before you ever get him to admit it."

"Do you really think he's crazy about me?"

"I guarantee it. But Brian's not a man who's willing to risk much emotionally. He has a pretty fragile psyche, and I think he's worried about your possible rejection if he makes a total commitment."

Deseret mulled Betty's evaluation, then said, "The kind of strength he has in other ways, you just don't think of Brian as weak in any way."

"I doubt that he considers it a weakness. For him it's just a matter of self-protection."

Deseret sighed. "I wish he was as concerned about protecting himself physically. He seems to think he's invincible."

"I can assure you he doesn't think of himself in that manner. He worries about dying just like the rest of us. He doesn't think of himself as being mortal."

"You knew his ex-wife, didn't you?"

"Not that well," Betty said, "but I knew her. She's a good person, which is what Brian would tell you. He didn't love her, but he feels guilty about the years he took from her."

"She took those same years from him," Deseret said.

Betty laughed. "You're going to have to quit being so defensive about Brian. A little mental suffering and guilt might be good for him."

Deseret smiled. "Sorry about that. I guess I'm a little too motherly."

"I'd be careful. I'm not sure Brian can handle your protectiveness."

"I'm so worried about him," Deseret said with a frown. "You know he's going to Oklahoma tomorrow."

"Yes, Dave and I are worried about him, too. But like any man, he has to do what he thinks is best. Otherwise, he'd have trouble living with himself."

"He's exposing himself to tremendous danger."

"He's in tremendous danger right here."

"I know, but if he'd only get some help."

"You might as well forget that. He's afraid of getting someone else hurt."

The waiter brought their food. They ate, continued discussing Brian's trip across the Red River, and expressed worry. After they had finished, Deseret stoutly proclaimed, "Damn it, I'm so depressed I'm going to buy out Neiman-Marcus."

"Thata girl," Betty said with a laugh. "A half dozen new outfits will chase all that depression away."

They laughed together.

Foster Cerney remembered Brian Stratford as a young, brash and strong-willed CIA operative in Vietnam. He knew Stratford was bulldog-like in terms of tenacity, felt fortunate the man hadn't been assigned to his case until the final countdown for the end of the ill-fated war.

Had Stratford had more time, Cerney thought the operative might have made things uncomfortable for him and his cohorts. Of course, if Stratford had caused problems, we would have killed him and he wouldn't be making a nuisance of himself now, Cerney thought.

Cerney remembered Stratford only after his lover Shelia Reichman, playing the role of Reginald Masters's sister, telephoned and told him about the journalism professor visiting her at the dead dean's home. Immediately, on recognizing the name, he ordered Shelia to make a hasty retreat.

Cerney blamed himself, to some extent, for not knowing Reginald's colleagues at the university. He promised himself that he would not make the same mistake twice.

Of course, the very idea of a former CIA operative working at the university with Reginald had never crossed his mind. In retrospect, he now remembered that Reginald might have said something about a man suspected of CIA connections working at the university. But a name hadn't been mentioned, and Reginald was such a scared and cowardly sort that he often dismissed anything the man said as merely fear speaking.

There wasn't much about Reginald to like, but he was loyal and he had done a good job for the organization. With all the money Reginald had been making, it was hard for Cerney to believe that he would take his own life. Again, there was all that fear in the man. Maybe it finally just did him in.

Reginald's death had caused the organization some problems, and more than just finding a replacement for the Dallas area. He had been the banker, the man counted on to launder money and make deposits in special accounts. He had been good at his job.

When Shelia called and said she couldn't find his book, when she said Stratford had visited her at Reginald's house, it didn't take Cerney long to theorize that the professor had been there previously and had taken the book.

While he was certain Stratford would not be able to properly decode the book, even with the help of CIA friends, he wanted it back. Cerney was a cautious man, not one to take unnecessary risks. It was one of the reasons, he told himself, that he had been so successful.

The names and other information in the book had been prepared, in the event of theft or loss, to lead anyone trying to decode it on a false trail. The decoder was to think the book was a record of dealers, distribution points, dates for shipment and costs. It was actually a book detailing numbered bank accounts in various countries.

In theorizing that Stratford had the book, Cerney also figured he would not immediately turn it over to a law enforcement agency, and possibly never do so. Cerney considered one of his major strengths to be that of knowing his enemies better than they knew him. In 'Nam, he'd developed an excellent profile on Stratford.

The man was a lone wolf, didn't trust anyone other than himself to do a job right.

Cerney was also sure that Stratford's emotions would get in his way. His profile showed the man to be volatile, often irrational, and extremely dangerous. What baffled him was why a man like that was teaching at a university.

At first, the book was the most important thing in Cerney's mind. After Shelia's failure to obtain it, he had checked with some of his law enforcement associates, and they assured him the book had not been turned over to local, state or federal authorities.

Cerney was a man who covered his tracks well, who paid high prices for the right people in the right places. Because he had been willing to pay the cost to do business, he had been able to remain in the shadows. He spent a week or two of each month at his Oklahoma retreat, the rest of the time on the French Riviera or some other exotic place.

His operation had brought him power, untold wealth, everything of which he had ever dreamed.

Now, all of a sudden, one man wanted to rob him of all he had worked so hard to obtain. Though Stratford was just one man, he had become a festering sore that wouldn't dry up and go away.

Fortunately, Reginald had kept a second book that was identical with the one in Stratford's possession. Once Cerney had it, along with assurances from his law enforcement associates that the other book had not been turned over to authorities, he wanted Stratford's head. His associates told him if Stratford did turn the book over to any law enforcement authority, they would be able to destroy it.

Of course, Cerney was sure no second-rate law enforcement agency would be able to decipher the book anyway.

So, all that was necessary to getting things back in order was the death of Brian Stratford. Cerney had already eliminated the Beckers, just on the chance that they might have caused some problems. They had been new to the business anyway, of very little value to him.

"Anything in particular you want to watch on television?" Shelia asked.

Cerney was stretched out in an oversized leather recliner, nursing a drink. He was wearing silk pajamas and a designer terrycloth robe.

"Whatever you want to watch is fine with me," he said, then laughed and continued, "just so it's not one of those shows where the police are brilliant and the criminals so stupid."

Shelia smiled. "Maybe we should just listen to some good music."

"Fine with me. Whatever you want."

She got the stereo going, loaded it with soft, instrumental music. She then positioned herself in the recliner next to his and asked, "Are you worried?"

"About what?"

"You know, Brian Stratford."

"Why should I worry about him?"

"You think he's coming after you, don't you?"

"Oh, he'll be coming all right, but the day he crosses the Red River he's a dead man."

She sighed. "I wish I could have taken care of it in Dallas. I don't like the idea of him coming here. If only I had —"

He interrupted. "It's not your fault. You had some good men working with you, but they got careless and he wasted them. He's the typical CIA type, though. He can't think without a weapon in his hand, and he thinks he's the Lone Ranger. I've got twenty-five good men working for me, so there's no way he can get me."

"You've told me many times that anybody can be hit," she said.

Cerney chuckled. *"You don't understand this man. He's one of those old-fashioned types who believes in letting the other guy draw first. He's a movie star hero cowboy from the word go. He's not going to sneak up behind me."*

"Still..."

"Don't worry, Shelia. Like I said, I've got twenty-five good men, and he's just one man."

"If I'm not mistaken, most of those twenty-five good men are South Vietnamese," she said, *"and the war proved their fighting abilities are a bit suspect."*

Cerney laughed again. *"They're fighting for real money now, not some stupid national cause."*

"Regardless of what you say, I'm worried. You don't mind if I worry a little bit, do you?"

He motioned for her to join him in his chair, and when she did he kissed her lips lightly. She was, he thought, a good woman. She had stuck by him through thick and thin, put up with his scores of brief affairs without so much as a murmur. He knew she didn't like for him to see other women, but she tolerated it because she was afraid of losing what little they had together.

"Why don't you build us a drink?" he said, handing her his empty glass.

She smiled. *"Is that all you want?"*

He returned her smile. *"For now."*

Cerney watched in silence while she walked to the bar, made two drinks and returned. After handing him his glass, she sat on the bearskin rug in front of the fireplace *and watched the flames lick and leap up from the logs. It was a peaceful, soothing time. Even though the room was large, the fire and furnishings gave it an aura of warmth and coziness.*

They sat drinking, watching the fire, listening to the music. The atmosphere was one of quiet melancholy.

Finally, she broke the silence. "The man, Stratford, do you know when he's coming?"

"Tomorrow," he replied. "My informants tell me he'll be coming tomorrow.

Shelia Reichman had been in love with Foster Cerney for almost twenty years. When she first met him, he was an army captain, and she was an eighteen-year-old secretary working on the base where he was stationed.

He was the first and only man she had ever loved. From the very first, his wish had always been her command. Though she had received a staunch Catholic upbringing, even graduated from parochial school, Cerney could make her forget all the morality preached and practiced by her parents.

She was totally, completely, his slave.

Early in their relationship, she realized he was a man committed to achieving wealth, no matter what the cost in human suffering. He had dabbled in the sale of narcotics when she first met him, but his involvement intensified to epidemic proportions when he was sent to Vietnam.

Shelia had not only waited patiently for his return, she had also served as a conduit for his illegal activities. Early on, he had taught her much about his business, knowing she could be trusted completely.

One of the things he had taught her was sell, never use the stuff. She never had. Cerney had told her the ones who used it were stupid and suckers, the ones who sold it were smart. And he adhered to his own advice.

Though Shelia had wanted marriage, a home and children, Cerney never mentioned matrimony. He liked having her with him for convenience, but he also liked his freedom. She was afraid to press for any of her own wants, likes and needs.

It was a one-way relationship, but she had grown comfortable with it.

When Cerney bought the ranch in Oklahoma, Sheila thought it might mean a slowing down, the beginning of a more tranquil life. But he now seemed even more restless, even more determined to build a stockpile of money. There was already enough, she thought. More, really, than they could spend in a lifetime.

Cerney was always brooding, planning, grasping for more. His traits weren't, for the most part, admirable, but her love overlooked them. It even overlooked his trips abroad without her, and his involvement with numerous women.

He explained that he couldn't take her on trips because he needed her at home, to make sure the business ran smoothly.

Though she could never tire of Cerney, she was getting tired of the business, and of what it did to people. Now this Brian Stratford has risen from the past, a man she feared because of both premonition and deed. From her limited experience with him, from what Cerney had said about him, the man seemed unstoppable.

Of course, Cerney planned to stop him. He also seemed to be enjoying the possibility of an encounter with Stratford, even anxious for it.

Shelia had great confidence in Cerney; thought he could adequately deal with just about any situation. She worried about people with causes, people on crusades. Ordinary methods didn't always stop such people. Such methods hadn't stopped the Viet Cong or the North Vietnamese.

She questioned whether or not Stratford could be stopped.

But then she told herself, he's just one man. One man against twenty-five. What can he do?

Still, she worried.

Cerney was in bed beside her, sleeping soundly. If he was right, the new day would bring Stratford to their world. She couldn't sleep for thinking about it.

19

The drive from Dallas to southeastern Oklahoma is normally relaxing, especially on a crisp, fall morning. Friday morning, however, found me extremely tense, more on edge than I had anticipated being.

Thursday night had been one continuous argument with Deseret. She had verbally barraged me, questioned my intelligence for not soliciting help in going after Cerney. I tried to explain to her that my first trip would merely be a reconnaisance mission, but she wouldn't listen.

Of course, it was something of a lie, since I had no idea what my first trip into Cerney country would entail. I was, however, prepared for the worst.

Anyway, she had tricked me into seeing her, wanting to show me some new clothes she had purchased at Neiman-Marcus. One look at the stuff, a wild guess on what it cost, and I again realized I'm not in the same financial league her dad is in.

My trip took me north on Highway Seventy-Five, then I took One Twenty-One east just past McKinney. At Paris, I took a farm road that intersects with Highway

Thirty-Seven, just before it crosses the Red River. Highway Thirty-Seven leads into Idabel, Oklahoma.

The trip, which I've made many times before for the purpose of fishing Lake Broken Bow, offers some beautiful scenery. I can never pass through Bonham or Honey Grove, two small Texas towns, without envying the people who live in such quiet, peaceful surroundings. I often stop for coffee at a small restaurant in Honey Grove.

On this particular day, I had too much on my mind to think about the scenery or a cup of coffee at Honey Grove. Of course, for much of the trip it was too dark to see the scenery. I had left Dallas at five o'clock in the morning, knowing the journey would take a little more than three hours.

Rex Chandler, who's a pharmacist, had promised to meet me at his drugstore in Idabel at eight-thirty.

Rex and I go back to 'Nam, where he was a captain in charge of a bunch of grunts, who are foot soldiers for those unfamiliar with military jargon. Anyway, on one occasion he and his boys saved my rear end. We became friends, checked out a few of Saigon's better night spots together. We were usually joined by Rex's twin brother, Paul, who is a doctor. That's what he was doing in 'Nam, patching up the guys who couldn't get out of the way of enemy fire, and sometimes our own.

Rex and Paul were the best friends I had in Vietnam, and I'd kept up with them over the years. They were both born in Broken Bow, Oklahoma, where Paul practices medicine. Broken Bow is just twelve miles from Idabel.

I figured that if anybody had a line on Cerney, it would

be the Chandler boys. I didn't plan to involve them in the Cerney project, just get a little information. Rex told me he was going to have Paul meet us at the drugstore, then we'd go have breakfast and swap a few lies.

As I topped a hill on the outskirts of Idabel, I saw some vehicles parked on the shoulder of the road and people milling around them. The natural inclination was to slow down, which I did. On doing so, I recognized those who had formed the waiting convoy.

Damn, I thought. I'm not believing this.

I pulled over and parked in front of the lead vehicle, got out of the Ramcharger and was greeted by eight grinning faces.

Frowning, I asked, "What in the hell are you people doing here."

"We're just on a reconnaisance mission," Deseret teased.

"Yeah," Bubba said, "just thought we'd come up and check out the country."

I turned to Dave and asked, "Are you responsible for this?"

Dave grinned and said, "Betty and I just happened to run into these folks. We were on our way to Beavers Bend State Park for a little rest and relaxation."

Dave was now acting chairman of the journalism department. I had asked him for Friday off, had asked him to get someone to fill in for me.

"And you," I said to Mark Lightfoot, "this is a little out of your jurisdiction, isn't it?"

The detective shrugged his shoulders. "I was just out for a morning drive and ran into these folks."

They were all getting a good laugh out of the situation; Honey and Alan in safari outfits, looking like they'd just stepped out of a display window at Abercrombie and Fitch; Chi Chi Knockers, wearing pants that had to have been painted on her, a low-cut sweater that left nothing to the imagination and a rabbit-skin jacket; fashion-conscious Betty in what had to be an Anne Klein outfit; and Deseret in designer jeans, a flashy sweater and a fox jacket.

Dave, Bubba and Mark were at least more appropriately dressed. Dave was in Marine Corps leftovers, Bubba in Army surplus camouflage, and Mark in jeans, sweatshirt, and jacket.

I sighed. "Well, follow me into town and we'll at least get some breakfast."

Deseret joined me in the Ramcharger and I led the other four vehicles into downtown Idabel. We parked in front of Rex's drugstore. I asked the others to wait in their vehicles while I went in.

Rex and Paul were waiting. They greeted me warmly, we did a little back-slapping, then Rex said, "This Cerney guy you want a line on, what's going down? You were kind of vague when we talked on the phone the other day."

"I'll fill you in later," I said. "Right now there are a few complications. Some friends decided to join me here. They weren't invited, but I guess we'll have to take them to breakfast."

"How many friends?" Paul asked.

"Eight."

"Damn," Rex said, "you've got a regular army."

"Once you see them, you won't think they're much of an army. Four of them are women."

I took the twins outside and introduced them to everyone. Rex pulled me aside and whispered, "That Chi Chi, she's built in the front like a fifty Studebaker."

"She's impressive," I replied in a soft voice, "but I wouldn't look at her too long or hard. Bubba and I had a fight because he thought I was looking."

"Really?"

"Yeah, really."

Rex and Paul rode in the Ramcharger on the journey to the restaurant. The waitress had to pull three tables together to accommodate the group.

"Your girl," Paul told me when no one could hear, "she's fantastic looking."

"She's fantastically young," I responded.

Breakfast was a time of lighthearted banter, with Rex and Paul getting to know the entourage from Dallas, and vice versa.

Rex, never the most discreet person in the world, started telling about a particular place he, Paul and I had frequented in Saigon. "You wouldn't believe what the girls there would do. They would —"

I interrupted. "I'm sure no one is interested in what we did in Saigon."

"I find it very interesting," Deseret said.

"So do I," Betty concurred.

"I'm more interested in Foster Cerney," I said. "I want all of you to hear what Rex says about the man, then you can all go back to Dallas."

My statement caused a general outbreak of laughter.

"Ever get the idea you're not in control?" Paul asked.

I lamented, "All my life."

"There's not much to tell," Rex said. "Cerney bought a small ranch near here a few years ago, and from what I can find out he's been a model citizen. He makes charitable contributions, supports the schools and Little League. Of course, I was in the dark in checking on the man since I don't know what he's supposed to have done."

"Since everyone else here knows, I guess you might as well know, too," I said. "I think Cerney's one of the biggest drug dealers in the southwest."

Rex and Paul took on an incredulous look, then Paul doubtfully said, "Operating out of southeastern Oklahoma?"

"Why not?" I asked. "Can you think of any better place to hide out?"

"To tell the truth, no," Rex said. "All of eastern Oklahoma was a pretty good place for outlaws to hide out before the turn of the century, but now..."

"There's been a lot of talk about marijuana being grown in the clearcuts around here," Paul said, "but I haven't heard much talk about the hard stuff."

The reference to clearcuts had to do with areas where timber companies were totally eliminating trees from forest lands.

"That's not just talk about the marijuana," Rex said. "There are a lot of law enforcement people around here who spend a considerable amount of time trying to locate marijuana farms, then destroying what they do find. The problem is that there are too few law enforcement people and too much land."

"What about your chief of police, your country sheriff?" Lightfoot asked.

"Good people," Rex said, "but spread a little too thin."

Surprised by Lightfoot's question, I said, "I figured you'd already checked out the local police chief and the sheriff."

"I didn't think it was a good idea," the detective said, "because I thought Cerney might have them in his pocket."

"Good point," I replied.

"The chief and the sheriff really don't know Cerney," Rex said. "I checked with them. I couldn't find anyone who really knows him. He keeps to himself and is gone most of the time. There's some lady who handles almost everything for him."

I described the phoney Julia Wood to Rex, asked him if the woman who handled things for Cerney looked anything like her.

"It sounds like one in the same," he said. "The name people here know her by is Shelia Reichman."

"I'm sure Cerney is dealing in marijuana," I said, "because he's not one to turn his back on a buck from any source. But his major bread is coming from the hard stuff."

"Where's he getting it?" Paul asked.

"Well, he has a lot of oriental connections, but I'm sure he also has sources in Central and South America."

"Whew!" Rex exclaimed. "I really didn't expect anything like this when you called. It sounds as if you know this Cerney character pretty well."

"Well enough," I replied. "He was my last assignment in Vietnam. I then proceeded to give the entire group all the sordid details about Foster Cerney.

"I can't recall you ever mentioning the guy in 'Nam," Paul said.

"You and Rex had already been shipped back to the states when I got the assignment."

Rex, mulling all that had been said, offered, "I doubt that anyone around here has a clue as to who Cerney really is. Folks know he has money, but he's obviously wanted privacy and no one I know of has infringed on it."

"Where's this ranch of Cerney's?" I asked.

"It's on Little River," Paul said.

"It's small, you say?"

"Just a thousand or so acres," he replied. "He's got a mansion of a house setting on it. He even has his own airstrip, hangars, and that sort of stuff."

I mused, "And I'll bet he has some helicopters and twin-engine aircraft."

"He's also got a jet," Rex said, "either a Lear or a Falcon."

"With his house and ranchland, what kind of layout are we talking about?" I asked.

"Formidable," Paul volunteered. "You've got the river on one side and heavy timber and undergrowth surrounding the rest. There's one road in to the house, and the place has some really elaborate fencing. There are guards, too, all Vietnamese."

"Hmmm," I said thoughtfully. "One road, huh? That means his only other way out is by air or the river."

Bubba grinned. "I like the way you think, Brian."

"How's he thinking?" Alan asked. "I'd like to know."

"We'd all like to know," Deseret said.

Dave laughed. "Not me. The one thing I can do without is knowing how Brian thinks."

"You're smarter than I gave you credit for being," Lightfoot said to Dave with a chuckle.

"It doesn't matter what I'm thinking," I grumbled. "All you clowns are going back to Dallas anyway."

"Right," Bubba said, rolling his eyes.

"I'll be right behind you, Bubba," Lightfoot said.

"Me, too," Dave chimed in.

"Well, Honey and I aren't going anywhere," Alan stated defiantly.

Rex laughed. "It doesn't look like you're in command here, Brian."

"I hadn't planned to be in command of anyone other than myself," I said.

"Do you think we ought to let the sheriff know what's going on?" Paul asked.

"What's this *we* stuff?" I challenged.

"You don't think Rex and I are going to let you and your friends handle this alone, do you?"

"I would hope that all of you would leave well enough alone," I said. "As for contacting the sheriff, I don't have a shred of evidence to back up what I've told you about Cerney. I just know he's dirty, that's all."

"That's good enough for me," Rex said.

"Well, it shouldn't be. I don't want any of you involved in something that might not go down just right."

"Life's a cabaret," Lightfoot commented.

"What the hell's that supposed to mean?" I asked.

"I have no idea," was the reply.

Everyone started talking at once, about where to headquarter, about a plan of action. I became an observer, listening to a small, directionless army.

"Hold it," I loudly proclaimed. "I told you I came here to do a little reconnaisance work, and that's exactly what I plan to do. I want to get the lay of the land before I do anything."

"Sounds reasonable," Dave conceded.

"Rex, I'd like to check Cerney's place from the air. Do you think I can rent a plane at the local airfield?"

"I've got a plane," Rex said. "It's a little slow, but it's dependable."

"What is it?"

"It's an old yellow biplane, a Stearman," he replied. "It was a Navy trainer in nineteen thirty-eight or thirty-nine."

I was familiar with the aircraft, popular with crop dusters.

"Good," I said. "I can handle one of those without any trouble."

"Whoa," Rex challenged. "I'll fly it. You observe."

"I need you and Paul here to ride herd on these malcontents," I said. "I think it'll be better if I go alone."

"And I think it'll be better if I go with you," Deseret said.

"I wish you wouldn't," Honey said to her daughter.

"I'm going," was the response.

"The hell you are," I said.

"The hell I am," she defiantly responded.

Betty laughed. "Please, no lovers' quarrel."

A lot of talk, some yelling, a little arguing, and the group decided Deseret would accompany me. Things were totally out of control. Another decision reached was that the rest of the troops would headquarter at the Holiday Inn and wait for our return.

Rex drove Deseret and me to the airfield, but before we left Bubba got an Uzi submachine gun out of his Suburban and gave it to Dez, along with plenty of ammunition.

"Where in the hell did you get that?" Lightfoot asked Bubba. "Never mind, I don't want to know."

Bubba grinned. "I got enough for everybody here who wants one."

Bubba is, indeed, a man of many surprises.

20

Foster Cerney had been waiting on the phone call since about eight-thirty. That's when he had received the first call, the one telling him Brian Stratford was in Idabel. This call told him Stratford was at the local airfield, that he was obviously going to be doing some flying in an old yellow Stearman.

That Stratford had obtained an aircraft didn't surprise Cereny. He had halfway expected the man to use a plane to check the lay of the land. It's what he would do, given Stratford's intent.

He went into the kitchen where the Vietnamese cook was busily preparing what would be lunch, plopped his massive six-foot–four-inch frame into a chair at the breakfast table. Shelia was already seated there, drinking a cup of coffee and reading a magazine.

She looked up and asked, "Do you want some coffee?"

"Yeah," he said.

His steel blue eyes followed her admiringly as she got up and poured a cup for him. October sunlight filtering through drawn curtains cast enough light to penetrate the light robe Shelia was wearing, outlining her supple and beautiful body.

After Shelia brought him the coffee and seated herself, he ran a hand through his mane of white hair and said, "He's here. He's on his way."

Shelia's eyes clouded, and almost fearfully she asked, "What are you going to do?"

He laughed. "Whatever's necessary. There is a development I hadn't figured on. His little girlfriend's with him. I didn't think he'd expose her to danger."

"He probably doesn't have a choice in the matter," Shelia said. "The girl's fiesty, strong-willed. I don't think he can control her."

"Well, if she gets in the way, she'll buy the farm just like Stratford. The only problem is, her death could cause us some problems. I don't think many people give a damn about Stratford, but from what you've told me she's from a wealthy family. Her family might be willing to pay to get some answers, which could cause us a little grief."

"Let's pray she doesn't get in the way," Shelia said. "We've had a nice, quiet life here, no one bothering us."

Cerney chuckled. "What's this let's pray stuff? Are you reverting back to your childhood, Shelia?"

She blushed, then stammered, "Just a figure of speech."

"There's been no reason for anyone to bother us here," he said. "We've given to the right causes, donated to the right political factions. We haven't given anyone reason to think we're anything other than wealthy people who've retired to southeastern Oklahoma to live the good life. I haven't had to pay one red cent to a crooked law officer or politician."

"People are suspicious of us," Shelia countered.

"People are suspicious of anyone with money," he said.

She disagreed. "I think it's all the Vietnamese you employ, not the money."

"Is the chicken processing plant at Broken Bow under suspicion?" he asked with a laugh. "They hire a lot more Vietnamese that I do."

"You know what I mean," she said with a smile. "The Vietnamese at the chicken plant act a lot more passive than our people."

"Well, some of my people have been with me a long time. They know how I want things done. They're soldiers."

"They're thugs," she argued.

"Tell me, would you rather have a chicken plant worker or one of our people between you and Stratford?" he asked.

She shrugged her shoulders. "You know the answer to that."

He glanced at his watch, drained the last of the coffee from the cup and said, "I'd better go down to the hangar and check on our preparations for Mr. Stratford. By the way, did I tell you some other people came from Dallas with him?"

"No, you didn't mention it."

"Nothing to worry about. Four guys and three women in addition to his sweetie. They had breakfast with a couple of local guys who've been asking questions about me. We may have to deal with them after we've taken Stratford out. Surprises me, though. My book tells me Stratford's a lone wolf."

"Maybe he didn't invite them," she said. "He has some loyal friends."

"Could be," he agreed.

At the hangar area, Cerney checked out the two choppers and crews designated to take care of Stratford. He figured one helicopter and only minimal firepower would be necessary to take care of his adversary, but why take chances?

He chuckled to himself, wished that he could be in one of the copters to see the surprised look on Stratford's face. But that would be a stupid and unnecessary risk, even though the choppers could fly rings around the old Stearman that Stratford was piloting.

Too bad about the girl, he thought. From what Shelia had said, she was a real looker. He hadn't told Shelia his intentions regarding Stratford and the girl, but then, he really hadn't decided what he was going to do until he got the call. That's when he rang the hangar and told the helicopter crews to get ready.

In Vietnam, in several years of drug dealing, Cerney had never exposed himself to danger. He saw no need to do so now. It was too easy to pay others to take the risk of dying.

21

It had been some time since I'd flown a plane, and I'm not saying how long since I'd flown a Stearman. However, when a kid I got my first taste of flying in a Stearman crop duster, and possibly for nostalgic reasons I think of the old biplanes as representing the best in pure aviation.

Of course, the dynamics of the plane are not what you'd call ideal. Rex's plane was one of the old style, commonly referred to as a "tail dragger." The main wheels were up front, well forward of the center of gravity, and there was a small tailwheel at the rear.

There are some obvious disadvantages to such an arrangement. In the three-point attitude, as it sets on the ground, the pilot is unable to see directly in front of the plane and thus must zigzag from side to side as he taxis. Turning is difficult without brakes or a steerable tailwheel, and the craft tends to weathervane in a crosswind.

Taking off requires balancing on the two main wheels while gaining speed. Landing, which I didn't really want to think about, requires that all three wheels touch the ground at the same time to prevent ballooning back into the air. Directional stability is poor after landing, which can lead to damaging "ground loops" if the pilot is negligent while rolling to a stop.

The inability to see directly in front of the plane has occasionally led to landing accidents.

Of course, all of the aforementioned problems were eliminated by the tricycle landing gear. But no matter what its problems, I love the old Stearman.

"Are you sure you can fly thing thing?" Deseret asked.

"Piece of cake," I said.

Rex laughed. "The engine may sputter a bit, but it's in pretty good shape. I had it checked out a few years ago."

He was kidding, of course, and Deseret saw right through him. "I'm not changing my mind, Rex. Neither one of you can scare me."

"I'm not even trying," I lamented. "I know it wouldn't do any good."

"Do you want to wear my old leather aviator cap and goggles?" Rex asked.

"Sure, why not?"

Rex reached in a bag he'd brought along and handed me the items, then he handed Deseret a cap and goggles, too. "It might be a little cool up there, and these goggles will keep the ducks out of your eyes."

Deseret laughed.

"Do you know how to use that Uzi?" Rex asked Deseret.

"Sure," she said. "Bubba gave me a quick lesson."

I shook my head in resignation. "Hopefully, she won't have to use it."

Soon the engine was purring. Then we were speeding down the runway, then rising into the air like a giant kite. The plane felt good to the touch, responsive.

I took a bearing north to Little River, then flew east along the waterway as Rex had directed. Except for the hum of the engine, it seemed quiet and peaceful in the sky. It was also cooler than anticipated, and the chill gripped me to the marrow of my bones. I worried about Deseret being cold, but there was nothing I could do about it.

Then I saw the house, just to my right. It was big, fortresslike. From the vantage point in the sky I could see the airstrip, hangar, and men scurrying about. What I didn't see, until it was too late, were two helicopters that suddenly swooped in on either side of the Stearman.

My immediate reaction was to take the plane up and into a loop, but such acrobatics didn't faze the pilots of the copters. They stayed with me, seemingly playing with me. I knew it wasn't play, though. It was a deadly game, with a death hand being dealt to the loser.

I went into a roll, but still couldn't shake the choppers. They were just too fast for the old Stearman.

Suddenly, Deseret had the Uzi pointed toward one of the copters and unloaded a few rounds. The pilot pulled away. She then trained the machine gun on the other helicopter and let go with a few short bursts. The pilot of that chopper, too, pulled away.

Both Deseret and I knew her machine gun bursts represented a temporary victory at best. The copters would be back, probably this time spraying us with automatic weapons fire.

I put the old Stearman into a dive, heard the engine

scream as the choppers converged on us again. A few bullets cut through one of the wings, but the plane held together. When it looked as though the nose was going to smash into the river, I pulled the plane out of the dive and flew along the winding river channel, so close to the water that the craft's wheels almost touched it.

The choppers were on either side of us, above the trees on the riverbank. I had the Stearman wide open, doing as much as I could with it to make us a difficult target, but there just wasn't enough in the engine to win against modern flying machines.

Bullets whined around us, tore through the body of the old plane. It was just a matter of time until we would be a confirmed kill. My mind was racing, knowing if we were shot down in the water we would be picked off like setting ducks.

Then it appeared, a clearing just to our right. I pulled the plane up out of the river channel and headed into the clearing, bordered on both sides by trees. I had already made up my mind that it was useless to try to outrun the choppers. My plan was to crash-land the Stearman, but in a place where we would have some cover.

I saw a small opening among some big trees and, flying no more than four or five feet off the ground, I took the plane in. Trees tore the wings from the craft as its wheels hit the heavy underbrush, and the main frame plummeted forward like a runaway train.

I'm not sure exactly what happened. All I know is that we were whizzing past trees and brush, then we were still. I was shaken and stunned by the impact.

My head cleared quickly, helped I'm sure by the noise

of the helicopters overhead. I quickly got out of what was left of the plane, then pulled Deseret after me. She was wide-eyed, but seemingly unscathed.

I grabbed the Uzi and the bag of ammunition for it, then grabbed Deseret's hand and headed for even denser cover. Fortunately, all the leaves had not yet fallen from the trees, so the choppers gunners were having trouble locating us.

My guess was that the choppers would be landed in the clearing, and the occupants would be coming after us on foot.

It was a damn good guess.

Dez and I took cover behind an old tree that had been uprooted by a storm, and she asked, "How many do you think there are?"

On impulse I kissed her tenderly, then said, "Four. We're lucky, baby, but I'd give anything if you weren't here right now."

She smiled. "I'm here because I wanted to be with you. And I'm glad I'm with you, no matter what."

I kissed her again.

When she took her lips from mine, she said, "It seems I've been waiting forever for you to be this affectionate, but do you think this is the best time and place for it?"

I chuckled. "Hell, I don't have a plan. I might as well be kissing you."

She put her lips to mine, kissed me long and passionately, then pulled away and said, "You'd better come up with a plan or we're history."

"The river's behind us," I said. "I want you to go upstream until you reach the highway. Then you'll be able to get help."

"And you?"

"I'll stay here and hold them off."

"I don't want to leave you."

"I don't want you to leave me, but the only chance either of us have is for you to get help."

She protested, "What you say makes sense, but —"

I interrupted. "You've got to go now. Time's running out. And take the Uzi. I've got my nine millimeter."

"I love you," she said.

"I love you, too."

She was suddenly gone, disappeared somewhere behind me. And there was a lump in my throat, thinking about how much she meant to me. She was a tough, tender, and smart lady. She realized what had to be done, and she didn't argue too much about doing it. She knew she might never again see me alive, but that I might survive if she got help. And she knew she was also exposing herself to danger in trying to get that help.

I appreciate people who don't flinch at responsibility, who do what's necessary to get the job done.

As for me, I was determined not to let any of the clowns in the helicopters get to her. If they did, it would be over my dead body. And me ending up as a corpse was a real good possibility.

While there were four of them, at least two with automatic weapons, I considered myself to have some advantages. First and foremost, they were looking for me, and they didn't know what to expect from me.

It was deja vu, Vietnam all over again, me hiding in the jungle and Viet Cong hot on my trail. And like it had been there, I was so scared it seemed my mind was running at the speed of sound. But it was the fear that made me most dangerous, more unpredictable, to my enemies.

Some Vietnamese are like some Americans, not worth a damn in a tight spot. Others are stealthful, dangerous jungle fighters, which are the types I figured made up Cerney's little army. They would be comfortable in the Oklahoma riverbottom.

I just hoped Deseret was making tracks. I calculated it couldn't be more than a couple of miles to the highway. Maybe I could buy her enough time to get there.

Then I heard another chopper. This one, too, set down in the clearing. Reinforcements. Cerney wasn't taking any chances.

What I needed to do was lead Cerney's men away from Deseret's trail upriver. If I could only get them to chase me downriver. That would mean, of course, crossing the clearing, where I would be exposed to their firepower for at least a couple of minutes. The odds of making it across the clearing were definitely not in my favor.

The alternative was to lead them across the river, then down it. But again, when crossing the river I would be an easy target.

If they got me quickly, Deseret certainly wouldn't be safe. I had to stall, to keep them at bay, to play for time. As to how I was going to pull it off, I didn't have a clue.

The clip in my nine millimeter held fourteen rounds. I had another loaded clip in my jacket pocket, along with maybe two dozen or so loose bullets.

Fifty rounds at most, I thought, not enough to engage in a full scale war, especially against automatic weapons.

On my belly, I snaked my way to the left, down toward the river. The only smart thing about having the river at my back was that it made getting behind me more difficult. Of course, if they approached me properly, it also eliminated retreat on my part.

I had no intention of retreating anyway.

Along the river's bank the undergrowth was fairly heavy, the trees mostly hardwoods. The foliage in the tops of the trees, painted by the season, was magnificently colored.

I knew that by now Cerney's men had examined the crashed aircraft, and that finding no bodies they would be coming after us. I had to let them find me, in order to allow Deseret to escape. I also had to put up a decent enough fight to give her the time necessary to get away.

A large tree had fallen into some heavy brush, so I laid down against it and waited. I didn't have to wait long.

The man was moving along the riverbank and directly toward me. He was moving quickly from tree to tree, using the big hardwoods for cover. To my right I saw another figure, then another. It was like a bad dream, never being able to get a fix on faces.

Except for the one man. I could see him clearly, and he was moving toward me, his Uzi at the ready position. He was now close enough for me to nail him with the pistol, but I waited.

Closer.

Closer.

He was suddenly almost on me, and I was springing from the ground like I'd been shot from a rubber band, smashing him flush in the face with the pistol. He squeezed off a wild burst with the Uzi, but then it was on the ground and so was he. I kicked him in the head for good measure, heard the sound of men yelling at each other, then felt the heat of bullets cutting through the brush around me.

I dived for cover, but only after retrieving the man's Uzi and his ammunition. With an automatic weapon in my hands, the odds were still bad but more favorable than they had been moments earlier.

One down and how many to go? There had to be a minimum of five more out there.

Now there was no human sound, only the soft rustling of wind caressing the treetops.

Deadly serenity.

I glanced at my watch. I figured if I could just hang on for thirty minutes, they wouldn't be able to catch Deseret.

It was easy enough to ascertain what was going on in the quiet. Now that they had located their prey, they were planning. And they would soon position themselves for the kill. They had the firepower and the manpower. I was a man in a box.

I searched my jacket pocket and found a pack of Trident sugarless gum, cinammon flavored. Normally I chew one piece at a time, but it being a special day and all, I plopped two in my mouth.

Hell, it was a nice day. If I'd had to pick a day in which to die, this one was as good as any, maybe even better than most.

It's funny what goes through your mind when your rear end's on the one, when you think it's all over except for that final unknown journey.

When the barrage of automatic weapons fire began, I knew what was taking place. It was covering fire for those moving closer to my position.

When in heavy fire, the tendency is to grab the ground with every part of your body, including the face. The enemy wants your eyes on the ground, not looking in his direction. It's hard not to fall into that trap.

Even with bullets making splinters of the fallen tree, throwing bark in my face, I forced myself to look. When any of my adversaries flashed through the standing timber, they had to dodge a burst from my Uzi.

I heard at least one scream of pain as a bullet found its mark.

Then I noticed blood on my right hand, wetting my trigger finger. I had been nicked in the right arm, but in the heat of battle hadn't noticed. I grabbed a handful of soft clay-like earth from underneath the log and slapped it on the wound. It stopped the bleeding momentarily, and the moment was all of life that I had to worry about.

They were closing in now, getting ever closer. I checked my watch, saw that it had been fifteen minutes since I'd last checked it. I wanted to give Deseret another fifteen minutes, but I wasn't sure I could hang on.

I thought about retreating even further, maybe even taking my chances in the river. I decided against it.

Things were getting fuzzy. My eyes burned from the bark and dirt kicked in them from flying bullets. When I saw a figure racing toward me through the trees, I leveled a burst at him.

He screamed, toppled to the ground.

Then everything was quiet.

Two down. It would give them something to think about.

I saw the man I'd downed crawling back in the direction from which he had come. I could have killed him, but it didn't seem important. He would be more trouble to his comrades wounded than dead.

They would regroup, which would burn a little more precious time off the clock. Every moment that passed gave Deseret just that much more of a chance.

After a few minutes the firing began again. Once again they began moving closer to me. I fired conservatively, only when I had a decent shot. I was dangerously low on ammo for the Uzi.

Then there was none.

I checked my watch. I had bought Deseret thirty-five minutes, but I was out of time and knew it. My pistol was no match for machine guns.

Since the enemy was seemingly trying to flank me, I decided to make a break up the middle. With bullets whispering their death message all around me, I came over the fallen tree, then started running swiftly through the timber.

For a few brief moments I thought I might be home free, but then I felt a jarring impact against the side of my head and toppled headlong onto the ground. Through blurred eyes I saw shadowy figures approaching me. One of them put a pistol to my head.

That's all I remember.

22

It took Deseret close to an hour to reach the highway and bridge crossing Little River. She had cried for much of the journey, tears of anger.

The first part of the trip had been one of quiet, of her fighting the brush, making her way through the trees. Then there had been the almost constant staccato sound of gunfire. There had then been a period of quiet again, causing her heart to pound wildly, causing the tears to rise like gushers into her eyes.

Strangely, there had been elation at hearing gunfire again, knowing that Brian was still alive.

For the past several minutes, though, she had heard nothing except the sound of automobile and truck engines grinding along the highway, of tires sucking and skimming along the roadway.

She was in surprisingly good shape for having traversed the rugged terrain along the river. Her jeans had stood up to the brush, and the fox jacket had protected the upper part of her body. There was a little dirt smudged on her forehead and chin, and her hair was a bit disheveled. After washing her tear-stained face with *river water, she thought she might be in good enough shape so as not to frighten passing motorists.*

At first, she started to leave the Uzi hidden near the bridge, knowing it might be difficult to thumb a ride with it in view. Then she decided to take off the fox coat and cover the machine gun with it.

The first vehicle coming her way stopped. It was an eighteen wheeler. The driver was a heavyset man with a pinch between his cheek and gum, a Texas Rangers baseball cap cocked back on his head.

"Where you headed, little lady?" he asked.

"Idabel," was the reply. "Do you pass by the Holiday Inn?"

"Sure do," the trucker said with a grin. "Would you like for me to stop and see if I can get us a room?"

She took the coat off the Uzi and the man's eyes widened. "I already have a room. You can just let me out there, and you just keep on trucking."

"Yes ma'am," he said. He had swallowed his snuff.

Bubba was the first person to see Deseret get out of the truck. He had been leaning against his Suburban, talking to Lightfoot and Dave. All three men rushed to her.

"Where's Brian?" Dave asked, the concern obvious in his voice.

She was all choked up, the hurt trapped in her throat like water in a reservoir. Finally, she gasped out, "Let me sit down and I'll tell you what happened."

Dave put his arm around her and gave support until they were in Alan and Honey's room. Lightfoot alerted the others and they also assembled there. Deseret sat on the edge of the bed, Honey and Alan beside her, trying to comfort her.

Then, between sobs, she told her story, ending it with, "Brian, he may be dead. My god, chances are he is dead." She started shaking, uncontrollably.

Dave, speaking softly said, "Hey, don't give up on Brian. The man can handle himself."

"We go in, we try to find him," Lightfoot said. "All you have to do, Dez, is give us a fix on the location."

She looked at the room full of people through teary eyes, then choked out, "I'll take you there."

"No, no, baby, that's not necessary," Alan protested. "We can find him. It's best that you stay here."

"There's no need for you to go," Honey assured. "The men can take care of it."

Deseret wiped the tears from her eyes with the back of her hand and defiantly announced, "I'm going. That's all there is to it. I know the way back, and I have to see for myself."

Honey sighed. "I wish you wouldn't."

"I have to."

"I know," Honey said, the resignation obvious in her voice.

"We need to move," Bubba encouraged. "And someone needs to call the Chandlers."

Betty volunteered, "I'll do it."

"Tell them to meet us at the river bridge," Deseret said.

"The women stay here," Lightfoot commanded, "except for Deseret. I think it might be a good idea for you to stay here, too, Alan."

"No way," the older man responded.

In Bubba's Suburban, it took the group only a few

minutes to reach the river bridge. Almost simultaneously, the Chandler twins arrived; Rex from Idabel and Paul from Broken Bow.

Bubba armed everyone in the party with Uzi machine guns.

"How many of these damn things do you have?" Lightfoot wanted to know.

"A dozen," Bubba replied with a grin.

Lightfoot shook his head in disbelief.

Dave, the Marine Corps training coming out in him, had more or less taken control of the operation. "I'll take the point. Bubba, you and Mark take the right flank; Rex, you and Paul take the left. Alan, you and Deseret bring up the rear."

For more than an hour they moved cautiously through the timber and along the river. It was Bubba who first spotted what was left of the yellow plane. From then on it was a matter of scouting the terrain, trying to piece together what had happened.

Rex found where Brian had taken his stand, also the blood from his wound. He kicked some leaves over the blood, so Deseret wouldn't know.

"He must have hit one of them here," Lightfoot called out, having found blood away from Brian's position.

Bubba came over and checked the spot, grinned and said, "He got two of them. I found some blood over there."

"Are you sure it wasn't Brian's?" Dave whispered.

"No way," Bubba assured. "Our man may be wounded, but he's not dead."

"How can you be sure of that?" Lightfoot asked.

"Sixth sense," was the reply.

When the group was all together, Dave said, "From what we've found here, we have to assume Brian's alive and that Cerney's holding him. I suggest we get on back to town and lay out a plan of action."

"I know Brian's alive," Deseret said. "I can feel it."

The men all looked uneasily at each other, hoping she was right but thinking the worst. They all made the trek back to the highway with thoughts rotating from optism to pessimism and back again, like windmills turning in their minds.

23

In my semiconscious state, I realized I was being dragged along the ground, pulled by my arms. The brush tore at my clothing. Fortunately, though, I was numb enough that I felt nothing.

A fist had hit me in the nose, and I sensed more than felt blood trickling over my lips and onto my chin. I couldn't taste the blood, but I knew some of it was getting into my mouth.

Vaguely, I could hear angry voices, cursing and shouting. The language wasn't American, but I'd heard it often enough in Vietnam. For a moment anyway, I was back there, knowing that the next breath I took might be my last.

Hands were hoisting my body into the air, tossing it roughly onto a hard surface. Then I heard the whine of a helicopter engine, a surge upward, and it was like my body was weightless and being shoved into space.

Helplessly, I listened to the sound of the engine, sensed the sensation of the chopper moving through the air. Then a boot hit me in the stomach, the air escaped my lungs, and there was blackness.

When I came to, I saw a blurry face above me, felt a cold cloth on my face. The face belonged to the phoney Julia Wood, the woman Rex said was called Shelia Reichman. I tried to raise myself up, but she pushed me back.

"Don't move," she commanded.

As my head and eyes cleared, I looked about the room and saw two men with Uzis. They both had their weapons trained on me, probably because I'd tried to raise myself up.

"Where am I?" I asked, already knowing I was somewhere on Foster Cerney's ranch. The question was more or less to hear my own voice. My mind was wondering about Deseret, whether or not she'd made it.

"Never mind," the woman said. "Just relax."

Easy for her to say. I felt like a herd of cattle were stampeding through my head. Maybe it was Deseret, leading the calvary to the rescue.

The room was austere. I recognized the platform I was lying on as an army cot. There were no sheets, just a mattress and a lumpy pillow without a pillowcase. Light filtered through a gauze-like curtain on a single square window. The exposed, bright light bulb, on the ceiling and above the cot, hurt my eyes.

"Where's Cerney?" I asked.

"Quiet," she cautioned. "You need some rest."

"Why. So I can die refreshed?"

She didn't say anything, but she didn't have to. Her eyes told the story. I was a dead man and we both knew it. As to why Cerney's boys hadn't finished me down by the river, that was something I didn't know or understand.

When she had finished cleaning me up, she rose to her feet and the guards came and tied me to the bed. They tied me well, too. There was no way I was going to get loose from the ropes.

"Tell me, where was I hit?" I asked. If Deseret had made it, she'd probably be in town by now. I hoped the rest of the men would be able to curb Bubba, to keep him from doing something stupid.

"A bullet grazed your head," she answered. "It left a pretty deep gash. There'll be a scar."

"I don't think I'll worry too much about it. By the time your boss gets through with me, a scar will be the least of my problems." Deseret, she'd probably think I was dead.

Shelia turned her face away from me. "You shouldn't have come here."

"Why? If I hadn't come here, he would have sent someone after me in Dallas. It doesn't make a helluva lot of difference where you die. You're just as dead one place as another. Besides, you would have killed me in Dallas, if you'd gotten the book."

"I've never killed anyone," she protested.

"Maybe you've never pulled the trigger, but those clowns who were holding the Antareses as hostages were under your orders. Are you telling me they wouldn't have killed us all if I'd delivered the book?" It would be best if my friends thought I was dead. Maybe, then, they wouldn't do anything foolish.

She tried to change the direction of the conversation. "We don't need the book anymore."

"Not needing the book won't stop the killing, will it? Dope dealers never tire of killing."

She ignored the statement. "I'll check on you again later." Then, she and the guards exited the room.

Though my head hurt like hell, I was getting rid of some of the cobwebs in my mind. I could feel my strength returning. Of course, no matter how much of my physical strength returned, there was no way I was going to get rid of the ropes binding me. If there were such a thing as a criminal merit badge for tying someone up, the two guards would have been shoo-ins.

Lying there on the cot, I had nothing better to do than to wonder why I was still alive. My mind reverted back to Roland, back to my childhood. Again, I wondered why he had been chosen to die, and not me.

Then the fever had me. I felt it burning, searing through me. It was frying my brain. Perspiration stood out on my forehead. My body became hot, sweaty. Then it was clammy and cold.

It had come and gone.

Quickly.

I wondered how I would handle death. I thought I would handle it well. There would be no begging. I'd go down with my chest out and my head held high.

Such thinking was not a matter of being macho or brave. If I'd thought there was a chance Cerney might let me live if I begged, I might have considered it. But if you're dead and know it, why give your enemy the satisfaction of seeing you crawl?

Lying there on the cot, staring at that damn glaring lightbulb, the perspiration now chilling me, I couldn't help but think about Dez. What we had was beautiful, very special. And here I was screwing it all up by getting myself killed.

Typical of you, Stratford, I thought. You're the epitome of a screw up.

In my mind I could see Deseret, recall our first glass of wine together, our first blueberry sundaes. Mentally, I felt myself smiling, though in reality I knew my teeth were clenched and my lips set. The pain in my head was no fun.

Visions started racing across my mind, of us sitting in the Ramcharger by the lake and watching the moon pop up like a giant orange balloon. I thought of what it would be like to be with her, of a world strictly our own, of touching, kissing and making love.

Then anger engulfed me, knowing that Cerney was going to rob me of the chance to be with Deseret; also knowing that I had by my own actions, perhaps, robbed myself.

It was not pleasant to think about.

I'm not sure how long my muddled thinking went on, since I had lost track of time. Someone had taken my watch, though bound as I was, I couldn't have seen it anyway. I only hoped the thief would have as many problems keeping it running as I'd had.

My thought processes were eventually interrupted by the return of the woman and the two guards. "Foster wants to see you," she said.

I didn't respond, just stared at her while one of the guards untied me. I was then dragged to my feet and shoved out the door and into the twilight. My legs were rubbery, but I was determined to stand straight and tall.

The room where I'd been kept was at one end of Cerney's aircraft hangar. The guards roughly pushed me into the front passenger seat of a Jeep, then hopped in back. One put the muzzle of his weapon against my head. The woman drove the vehicle to the big house, which was a considerable distance from the hangar.

I was herded into a large den where Cerney was waiting. He was standing in front of a native rock fireplace, a trophy whitetail deer head over its mantle. A fire was crackling and Cerney had a drink in his hand.

"Well, well, Mr. Stratford," he said. "Can I offer you a drink?"

"I'll pass."

He smiled. "I'd really suggest you have one. It might ease the pain."

"I'm not in any pain."

He gloated. "You will be. Do you handle pain very well, Mr. Stratford?"

I shrugged my shoulders. "Well enough, I suppose."

"Oh, I think you're too modest," he said. "I'm sure the Company taught you to handle pain very well."

"I don't know what you're talking about."

"Come, come," he teased, "you're not already going into your disassociation routine, are you?"

Cerney's reference was to mental control, of putting yourself in a state of mind that makes you unconscious to the pain of reality. It's an escape technique, which if mastered can enable you to endure tremendous torture. Mentally, you're just not there to feel the pain. But it's not the easiest of mental exercises to master.

I shrugged my shoulders. "I'd like to disassociate myself from this headache."

"Shelia, get Mr. Stratford a couple of aspirins and a

glass of water," Cerney ordered.

She obediently trotted off to do his bidding.

"Nice house," I observed.

"Yes, I noticed you've been looking the room over very carefully," he said. "But if you're thinking about the possibility of escape, my suggestion is that you forget it. You don't have a prayer. You're like a fly caught in a spider's web."

"Good analogy, but I don't think you expect me to just roll over and play dead."

He laughed. "No, playing dead is not what I have in mind for you."

Shelia came back into the room. I took the aspirins from her, plopped them in my mouth and drank the glass of water. Only then did I realize I hadn't had any liquid since early morning. No food, either.

"Since, to quote you, I don't have a prayer, would you mind answering a few questions for me?"

"Not at all."

Cerney was enjoying this, toying with me like a cat plays with a mouse before killing it. "About Reginald Masters, why did you have him killed?"

"I didn't," he said. "I was under the impression he committed suicide."

His denial surprised me. "And I suppose you're blameless in the deaths of the Beckers?"

"No, I'll take credit for Professor and Mrs. Becker. My reasons might be a little complicated for you, probably immaterial, too. But Reginald Masters was a very integral part of our operation. We miss him a great deal.

"Shelia, honey, would you please get me a refill?"

She got up from the couch and took his glass. I couldn't help but think that if she were a dog, she would be wagging her tail at the chance to serve her master.

Cerney was still standing in front of the fireplace, and I was standing about six feet from him. The two guards were standing a few feet behind me, on alert for anything I might try. One wrong move and my body would be like a sieve.

"I understand you no longer need the book," I said.

"That's right," he acknowledged. "We have a copy."

"Aren't you afraid that my copy will fall into the wrong hands?"

He laughed. "You mean in the hands of the police, of course?"

"Yeah, that's what I mean."

"I doesn't matter."

"It doesn't?"

He laughed again. "They'll never be able to decipher it. It will provide them nothing but false leads. Besides, I have friends in the law enforcement community. They'll see the book is never used."

His arrogance annoyed me, and I couldn't control the despair and anger that was building up inside me. I was going to buy the farm, and for what? Cerney would still be operating, still selling his poison.

There was plenty of buyers; stupid, mindless people who were anxious to pay so they could be used, so Cerney could be rich and so they could end up blubbering idiots.

"I'm sure you're wondering what's in store for you," he said.

"Not really. Dead is dead no matter how you hack it."

"I'm sorry you're not more concerned. Most people would have a preference as to how they died."

"Oh, I have a preference," I said. "I was hoping to die in bed of natural causes, and at a ripe old age."

"I think you've had a full life," he said. "My file on you shows that you had a very full and productive one."

"I didn't know you cared enough about me to keep a file on me."

"I started it in Vietnam," he informed, "but I haven't had much fresh material for it until lately. You see, Mr. Stratford, I keep a very wary eye on my enemies, try to know and understand them better than they know and understand me."

"It sounds like a good idea, but it must be very time consuming with the number of enemies you have."

"You'd probably be surprised," he said. "I probably have fewer enemies than you do. Money buys a lot of friends, and in high places."

"How many people have you bought at the university?"

He mulled the statement, then asked, "Tell me, Mr. Stratford, why did the CIA assign you to the university?"

It was my turn to laugh. "What in the hell are you talking about?"

"Come, come," he chided. "We know you're an operative. Were you assigned to the university to get to me through Reginald?"

"Sorry to disappoint you, Cerney, but I'm not an operative. I don't know who your sources are, but until Reg's death I had no idea about your whereabouts or about what you were doing. Of course, I knew that wherever you were, you'd be dirty. I don't think you know how to be any other way."

He laughed. "Still the righteous man, I see, right to the end."

"If being righteous is hating what you've done to a lot of people, of wanting to smash you for it, then I guess I'm righteous."

With a sneer, he replied, "Your attitude makes your going away party all the sweeter. You're going to enjoy an overdose of some of the finest stuff available. And when your body is found in Dallas, where we're going to take it, a lot of people are going to remember Brian Stratford as a junkie. That's how your children are going to remember you, how your students will remember you."

Cerney could have told me he was going to castrate me and tie me to an ant hill, and it wouldn't have bothered me as much as the knowledge that my children and students might remember me as a junkie. Of course, he knew that; knew how much I hated drugs, those who sold them and those who used them. What he proposed was, for me, the most terrible death imaginable.

My silence caused him to caustically ask, "What's wrong, Mr. Stratford? Does the cat have your tongue?"

I was sure I hadn't shown any loss of composure, though inwardly my heart was churning. "When's all this going to happen?" I asked, startled by the calmness of my own voice.

He again sneered and replied, "You'll have your first injection in the morning. I want you to have the entire night to think about it. I'd like to see if you're as mentally tough as you appear to be."

"Aren't you afraid someone will come looking for me?"

He laughed, derisively. "Not at all. What can four men and four women do against my people?"

At his mention of four women, I breathed a sigh of relief. Deseret must be alive. And he hadn't included the Chandler twins as being in the group that was a threat to him. That was good. They would have to continue living in this area after I was dead and buried.

"Maybe my friends will contact the police," I said.

"Let them. I'll claim I know nothing about you, and they have absolutely no grounds for harrassing me. As far as the law in this area is concerned, I've done nothing wrong."

"I've got to hand it to you, Cerney. You're a real piece of work. If slime were marketable, you'd bring a good price."

"Your bravado is commendable, Mr. Stratford. But let's see how well you hold up tomorrow."

"It'll take more than you to make me crawl."

"Your little girlfriend may not be so difficult."

"What do you mean?"

"Just something for you to chew on, Mr. Stratford. When I'm through with you, I think I'll take her. And when I'm through with her, maybe I'll sell her to some of my friends in Iran."

All along, I was sure Cerney was baiting me, trying to get me angry. His threat to Deseret was all it took to make me come unglued. Releasing all the pent-up rage in me, I charged him, thinking a bullet was a much better death than a needle anyway.

My lunge caught him by surprise, and the top of my head caught him flush in the nose. Blood spurted, and when I looked up and saw his face it was as if his eyes were going to pop out from surprise.

I aimed a killing blow at his neck, but before it landed the butt of a guard's weapon caught me on the side of the head and I crumbled to my knees. I was still conscious enough to hear Cerney yelling at the guards not to kill me.

He cursed me and yelled, "Tomorrow, I want you to think about tomorrow. Tomorrow is your day, and then it will be party time for your slut girlfriend."

I tried to get up, to again smash Cerney. But there was nothing left in my legs. Then I saw his boot coming at my face, and there was darkness.

24

It was Rex who suggested a sunrise attack on Cerney's ranch, though "attack" might not have been the best word to describe what the group was going to try to do. It was actually a rescue operation, one in which they would try to locate Brian and then get him out of the danger zone as quickly as possible.

The meeting in which Rex made his suggestion was conducted shortly after the men and Deseret had returned from their fruitless search for Brian. They were all convinced, or wanted to believe, that Cerney was holding Brian captive.

"The way we'll go in," Rex explained, "the sun will be to our backs and directly in the eyes of Cerney's people. I figure the six of us —"

Honey interrupted. "There are ten of us. None of us are staying behind."

Paul tried to protest. "But —"

"No buts," Betty said. "All the women have discussed it, and we go."

Rex and Paul looked helplessly at Alan, David and Bubba, all of whom merely shrugged their shoulders in resignation. Lightfoot, watching the proceedings, just continued chewing on his toothpick.

"What vehicles are we going to use?" Bubba asked. "We can use the Suburban, of course, but it's not the greatest attack vehicle in the world."

"We can use the Mercedes, too," Alan volunteered, "but I don't guess it's all that great either. What do we really need?"

"Ideally, Jeeps," Rex said. "But I don't have any friends who own a Jeep. I might be able to borrow a couple of pickups, though."

"Is there a Jeep dealer in this town?" Alan asked.

"Yeah," Rex said. "We have one."

"Well, get him on the phone and see how many he has," Alan commanded.

Rex hesitated momentarily, then asked, "What kind?"

"New ones," Alan said.

Bubba laughed. "Tell him C-J Sevens."

Rex telephoned and got the dealer, who was about to close his business for the day. After a few pleasantries and questions, he turned to Alan and informed him the dealer had eight C-J Sevens.

"I guess we'll need five," Alan said, looking at Bubba.

Bubba nodded agreement.

Rex told the dealer he wanted five Jeeps, and that he wanted them immediately.

"He says he can't have them ready before Monday," Rex informed the group.

"Tell him I'll pay his shop people a thousand dollars apiece if they'll get them ready tonight," Alan said.

Rex relayed the message, then said to Alan, "He wants

to know if you care how much the Jeeps cost?"

"Tell him I'll pay the sticker price, because we don't have time to haggle. And if he doesn't want to take a check, I can put all five Jeeps on American Express."

Betty marveled, "You can do that!"

"I can do that," Alan assured her.

Once the deal was cut, Bubba said he'd go work with the dealer's shop people to make sure the Jeeps were properly stripped down for action.

"I'll help you," Lightfoot said.

They got busy then, laid out all the details of their rescue mission.

Deseret lay wide awake on her motel room bed. She was certain Brian was alive. Though they were separated by distance and a bizarre situation, she thought she could actually feel the meshing of their minds together; also feel the touch of his hand as he reached out to her.

Worry furrowed her brow. She had argued for an immediate rescue attempt, thinking that the longer Brian was in Cerney's clutches, the greater the danger. And, of course, she was concerned that he might be hurt, possibly seriously wounded.

The others had tried to convince her that a rescue attempt, when they were so unprepared, would prove disastrous. But it was hard for her to think logically. She knew she wasn't thinking clearly, that she was too involved emotionally, but that still didn't make the delay any easier.

She had even suggested that they enlist the aid of local law enforcement, but that idea, too, had been shot down.

"Chances are that Cerney has Brian on the ranch,"

Lightfoot opined, "but if we send the sheriff out there to look for him, he might not find him and Cerney might move Brian to where we could never locate him."

Deseret thought the detective's assessment of the situation made sense, but she wasn't sure.

Local law enforcement had also been eliminated as a source of possible aid for the sunrise rescue mission.

"They wouldn't go along with something like that," Paul said. "What we're doing is against the law. We're enacting vigilante justice."

Rex did have a friend who was going to call the sheriff's office about the rescue attempt, at the exact time it began.

"If Cerney does have someone in the sheriff's office, it'll be too late for them to contact him," Rex explained. "More important, it'll be too late for the sheriff to get there to stop us. By the time he and his deputies get to the ranch, we'll either be victorious or it'll be our Alamo."

All of them were somber at the thought of possibly dying during the rescue attempt, with the exception of Bubba and Chi Chi. Bubba was anxious, and would have tried to get Brian out on his own if the others hadn't curbed him. And Chi Chi was preoccupied with doing her nails.

Deseret thought Chi Chi was nice, it was just that her elevator didn't run all the way to the top.

However, before she had gone to bed, Deseret and her parents had gone down to the car dealership to check on the progress being made in readying the Jeeps. There was Chi Chi, working right alongside Bubba, and getting just as dirty.

In fact, everyone in the group was working, so she,

Honey and Alan had joined in. Other than for Bubba, who seemed to know what he was doing, she wondered if for the rest of them the effort wasn't more therapeutic than beneficial.

The plan called for the women to drive the Jeeps, the men to ride shotgun with Uzis. In the case of the Chandler twins, Paul would be the driver.

She was proud that her father had so willingly purchased the Jeeps, that money hadn't even been a consideration. Referring to Brian, Alan had said, "The man saved all our lives. I wouldn't be here to spend the money if it wasn't for him."

Deseret wanted to sleep, wanted to be fresh for the morning, but sleep wouldn't come.

25

When I came to, I was not tied to the cot and there was no glaring lightbulb above me. Instead, I was lying on damp ground in almost complete darkness. A small sliver of moonlight was coming from what I guessed was a door.

Whatever help the aspirins Shelia had given me might have been, that help had been negated when the guard had clubbed me on the side of the head. I reached a hand up to where I'd been hit and it felt sticky to the touch.

Blood.

I'm not sure why, but except for the headache, I didn't feel all that badly. Maybe it was the adrenaline flowing, realizing what Cerney had planned for me, but I could feel the power returning to my limbs.

Mentally, anything resembling a logical solution to my dilemma that had been working in my mind had been replaced by anger. I had been shot, clubbed, thrown around like a sack of potatoes, kicked and hammered in the head with the butt of a gun.

And now they planned to use a needle on me.

Chances are they would succeed, but it wouldn't be

without a fight. They'd made a mistake in not tying me up again, because they were going to have to club me into submission. I was not going to be a willing subject.

After a thorough check of my surroundings, I ascertained that I was in an old storm cellar, probably built years before Cerney bought the land and built his big house. The place was full of spider webs and spiders, but they were the least of my worries. A bite from a brown recluse or black widow was of little consequence in comparison to Cerney's plans for me.

Through a crack in the wooden door at the top of the cellar's steps, the same crack that was letting the moonlight in, I could see a guard. Even with a locked door, and me beaten to a pulp behind it, Cerney wasn't taking any chances.

For maybe an hour, I really had no way of knowing how much time passed, I searched the floor and walls of the old cellar for something that would serve as a weapon. Spider webs clung to my face and hands, and occasionally a spider journeyed across my skin.

All I could find was an old nail.

I tried to take the steps apart with my hands, but the old lumber was like petrified rock. I couldn't budge it.

The nail would have to do.

I sat on the foot of the steps, put my hand against them, and tried to get some sleep. It wouldn't come. There was too little of my life left for me to waste it on sleep. The time would be better spent in recalling good memories.

I thought about Deseret. I thought about her a lot.

I tried to pray. I've never been very good at it, but figure God knows what I want to say.

The time didn't pass slowly. I don't guess it ever does when it's in short supply. The moonlight disappeared and the first light of day began filtering through the crack in the door. There were morning sounds, the distant sound of voices and motors grinding.

Then I heard the hum of an engine coming in my direction, and I guessed it was the Jeep coming to take me to the big house. I figured Cerney would want to play a few more games with me before ordering the fatal injections. I was his new toy, and he wanted to run its batteries down before discarding it.

The engine I'd heard died nearby, and I heard Shelia Reichman's voice giving orders to the guard. Then the cellar door was unlocked and opened, allowing the light of day to roll in. My eyes immediately picked up Shelia and two armed guards. With his weapon, one of them motioned for me to come up the stairs.

I hesitated, acted as though I couldn't see, in order to allow my eyes to become more acclimated to the light. When he was sufficiently irritated at my reluctance, I started up the stairs, the nail in one hand and a load of dirt in the other.

Of course, they had to know I'd try something, that I preferred a bullet to a needle. Cerney would have informed them of my probable mood. Anyway, as I neared the top of the stairs the guards began to back away, out of my reach.

Simultaneous with my emergence from the cellar, the sun exploded from the ground on the eastern horizon, setting some pastureland ablaze with light. From the sun came the roar of motors and the all too familiar sounds of automatic weapons being fired.

Shelia and the guards seemed stunned by the suddenness of the noise coming from the direction of the sun, and unmindful of me for a split second. It gave me a chance to charge one of the guards, throw dirt in his face as he turned back toward me, then drive the nail in his throat.

It didn't kill him, but blood spurted profusely and he loosened his grip on his weapon. As we tumbled to the ground, I was able to wrench the Uzi from him and turn it on the other guard. I spattered his chest as bullets from his automatic weapon dug divots in the earth around me.

Shelia started to reach for the fallen guard's weapon, but I loudly cautioned, "I wouldn't."

She retreated until her back was to the Jeep. I got up from the ground and checked the wounded guard. He wasn't going anywhere. He was too busy clutching his throat, trying to keep from bleeding to death.

Then I looked back toward the sun and saw Chi Chi driving a Jeep toward Cerney's aircraft hangar. Bubba was standing in the back, holding to a roll bar with one hand and, with an Uzi in the other, laying down a deadly field of fire.

And there was Honey, running a man down in the Jeep she was driving, pulling up alongside him so Alan could club him down.

I recognized the others then. Dez and Lightfoot, Dave and Betty, Rex, and Paul. They were all driving and shooting, hell-bent for leather, forcing Cerney's men to throw down their weapons or fall before their withering fire.

I forced Shelia into the passenger seat in the Jeep, and drove to where the action was taking place. By the time I arrived, it was all over. The group had six of Cerney's men face down on the ground, and Bubba was tying their hands and feet.

When I pulled up in the Jeep, Deseret was already out of hers and running toward me. We embraced, tried to kiss, but I yelled, "Ouch!" My lips were badly busted up, and suddenly they hurt like hell. In fact, my entire body felt as though it had been in the path of a bulldozer.

We laughed, joyously. Everyone was patting me on the back.

I remembered, then, and my mood blackened. "Cerney, he's in the house," I said.

"We'd better get the hell out of here," Paul said.

"No," I disagreed. "It ends here. It ends today."

"I'll take him," Lightfoot said, referring to Cerney.

"He's mine," Bubba argued.

"We all take him," Alan said.

I sighed. "I can't thank any of you enough, but I think all of you understand that I've got to do this myself."

The men nodded agreement, but Deseret said, "No, I don't understand that at all. You're hurt. We can all do this. If we all attack the house, he may surrender."

"Hey," Bubba said to Deseret, "a man's got to do what a man's got to do."

She grumbled, "You don't make a whole lot of sense, Bubba."

Chi Chi, who had been filing her nails, said, "Amen to that."

"We don't even know how many he has with him in the

house," Dave said. "He may have a dozen people up there."

"My count is four dead, five wounded and the six we have here who surrendered," Rex said.

"There's one dead and one wounded near the old cellar," I told them.

"How many people do you think he has?" Alan asked.

All eyes turned to Shelia. She looked at me defiantly, then spit on my face. Deseret walked up to her, gave her a hard look, then unloaded an uppercut that caught Shelia right under the chin. She fell to the ground like a rock.

"You bitch, if you want some more, I'll give it to you," Dez said.

From her position on the ground, Shelia said, "He has two. He has two more men with him."

All the action had taken place out of sight of the big house. Cerney had expected trouble, had put his men out to cover the road and other possible accesses to his fortress. That they had failed, had perhaps been too arrogant in their numerical strength, was obvious.

Even with only a couple of men in the house to support him, I didn't expect Cerney to be easy. And I didn't want any of my friends getting hurt. To this point, they had been very lucky.

I got in Shelia's Jeep and cranked it, then Deseret was alongside me. "You need a driver," she said.

I squeezed her hand. "Not this time, baby."

Honey came over, put her arms around Dez, and pulled her gently away. I went roaring off toward the house, hoping to at least get to the big trees in front of it before drawing fire. As I neared the trees, I planned to bail out and proceed on foot. I glanced behind me.

Five Jeeps were in hot pursuit.

My friends had snookered me. They had never had any intention of letting me try to take Cerney alone.

We didn't draw any fire, which surprised me. After everyone was in the trees, Dez at my side, we deployed and moved in on the house. The front door was suddenly thrust open and two men, their hands on their heads, came out.

We were about to enter the house, make a room to room search for Cerney, when I heard the noise at the airstrip. It was the sound of engines being fired up.

An escape route. Of course, Cerney would have one. I'd been stupid, maybe too angry to think logically. And now he was going to get away.

I bolted for the Jeep, Deseret at my heels. She was in the passenger seat by the time I had the engine started. Then I was racing back toward the airstrip, the other Jeeps right behind.

By the time I could see the runway, I knew it was too late. Cerney's plane was roaring down it, then rushing upward into the sky.

And then it exploded.

All the Jeeps were brought to a halt, and we all got out and milled around, puzzled at what had happened. Except for one.

"What happened?" Dave asked.

"I have no idea," I said.

Bubba grinned and said, "The ol' boy would've been all right if he hadn't raised his landing gear. When I was down at the airstrip, I rigged a couple of little charges in case someone decided to try to get away in the plane."

EPILOGUE

I'd been back at the university for a couple of weeks before deciding to deal with the person responsible for Reginald Masters's death. As far as Deseret and my friends were concerned, the killer was Foster Cerney. I saw no need to tell them anything different.

With Rex, Paul, and Lightfoot's help, my friends had walked away from the raid on Cerney's ranch with nothing more than a verbal slap on the wrist from the sheriff. He and his deputies were able to find enough evidence on the ranch to show the kind of major drug operation Cerney was running.

Of course, a repentant Shelia spilled her guts. Before she was through, I expected authorities to pin a sainthood medal on her for all she had endured under Cerney's magical spell.

It would have made everything a lot easier if Cerney had been the one responsible for Reg's death. It was something I didn't want to deal with, yet knew was necessary. So, I made the trek over to the office of the late Reginald Masters.

"Still no replacement, I see."

"I don't think they'll replace Dr. Masters until next semester," Martha Paul replied.

"Hell, I don't see much point in replacing him," I said. "You know more about running things than he did."

She laughed. "I'm just a secretary, Brian."

"No, I think you're much more than that, Martha."

"I don't know what you mean."

"Do you have any fresh coffee?" I asked.

"My coffee's always fresh," she assured. "Do you want a cup?"

"I would be most appreciative. And why don't you pour yourself a cup and join me?"

She poured the coffee, doctored mine the way she knows I like it, handed me the cup and took a seat behind her desk. I was sitting in a high-backed chair in front of her.

Our eyes met and she said, "You know, don't you?" There was a deep sadness in her face.

"Yeah, I know."

"How long have you known?"

"A week or so."

"What are you going to do?"

"I'm going to drink this cup of coffee."

"But what are you going to do about me?"

"You mean about you and your husband, don't you?"

"None of it was his idea. He didn't want to have anything to do with it."

"Well, if you're appointing me your judge and jury, I'm sentencing you to keep a good, fresh pot of coffee on all the time."

"You're not going to turn me in?"

"For what? For doing something that should have been done by a court of law? No way, Martha. Your family's been hurt enough. You just keep quiet, so no one else in your family will be hurt."